WOMEN HEARTS

Barbara Cartland

Barbara Cartland Ebooks Ltd

This edition © 2020

ISBNs

9781788673907   EPUB

9781788673914   PAPERBACK

Book design by M-Y Books
m-ybooks.co.uk

THE BARBARA CARTLAND ETERNAL COLLECTION

The Barbara Cartland Eternal Collection is the unique opportunity to collect all five hundred of the timeless beautiful romantic novels written by the world's most celebrated and enduring romantic author.

Named the Eternal Collection because Barbara's inspiring stories of pure love, just the same as love itself, the books will be published on the internet at the rate of four titles per month until all five hundred are available.

The Eternal Collection, classic pure romance available worldwide for all time .

THE LATE DAME BARBARA CARTLAND

Barbara Cartland, who sadly died in May 2000 at the grand age of ninety eight, remains one of the world's most famous romantic novelists. With worldwide sales of over one billion, her outstanding 723 books have been translated into thirty six different languages, to be enjoyed by readers of romance globally.

Writing her first book 'Jigsaw' at the age of 21, Barbara became an immediate bestseller. Building upon this initial success, she wrote continuously throughout her life, producing bestsellers for an astonishing 76 years. In addition to Barbara Cartland's legion of fans in the UK and across Europe, her books have always been immensely popular in the USA. In 1976 she achieved the unprecedented feat of having books at numbers 1 & 2 in the prestigious B. Dalton Bookseller bestsellers list.

Although she is often referred to as the 'Queen of Romance', Barbara Cartland also wrote several historical biographies, six autobiographies and numerous theatrical plays as well as books on life, love, health and cookery. Becoming one of Britain's most popular media personalities and dressed in her trademark pink, Barbara spoke on radio and television about social and political issues, as well as making many public appearances.

In 1991 she became a Dame of the Order of the British Empire for her contribution to literature and her work for humanitarian and charitable causes.

Known for her glamour, style, and vitality Barbara Cartland became a legend in her own lifetime. Best remembered for her wonderful romantic novels and loved by millions of readers worldwide, her books remain treasured for their heroic heroes, plucky heroines and traditional values. But above all, it was Barbara Cartland's overriding belief in the positive power of love to help, heal and improve the quality of life for everyone that made her truly unique.

AUTHOR'S NOTE

Dakar, which incredibly rapidly became the centre of French Colonial Society in the twentieth century, required a great deal of construction and public works to make the living conditions suitable for Europeans.

From a handful of European merchants and Company employees in 1900, the white population of Dakar rose to two thousand five hundred in 1910.

The high ideals of France's policy of colonisation and total assimilation in Senegal was helped by the increasing presence of European women.

There were over one thousand by 1926 and they all made a great impact on the domestic scene. There was a series of colonial handbooks dedicated to the problems of their activities and diversions. These included *Care of African Children* and *Studies of Flora and Fauna*. Evening dress was compulsory on most social occasions.

When I visited Dakar in 1979, I found it an impressive and beautiful City and a perfect holiday resort.

President Leopold Sedar Senghor, whose encouragement of black culture and art has had a huge effect in raising the status of the natives, is France's most famous modern Symbolist poet.

CHAPTER ONE
1899

Walking along the corridor, Kelda heard the sound of someone crying.

She paused, listened and realised that it came from the room of Yvette de Villon.

She stood still, controlling an impulse to knock on the door and ask what the matter was.

She well knew that it was not her job to interfere in any way with the older girls. Mrs. Gladwin had made that very clear when she had promoted her from being little more than servant doing all the odd jobs that nobody else would do to the position of Assistant Mistress.

"As you play the piano so well," she had said in the hard voice in which she spoke to her inferiors, "you will supervise the practising of the younger girls and you will also sit in the classroom when they are doing their homework. That will relieve the proper Mistresses."

She paused as if she was thinking what else she could pile on Kelda's shoulders and then added,

"Of course, your duties as regards the laundry, the sewing and mending will continue as before but you can look on this as a promotion and you should be suitably grateful."

"Thank you, madam," Kelda said automatically.

Mrs. Gladwin's eyes rested on her critically.

"I consider that gown to be too tight in the bodice. It is almost indecent."

"I am afraid I have grown out of it," Kelda replied apologetically.

"Then let it out!"

"I have done that already, madam."

"Excuses, always excuses to spend money," Mrs. Gladwin exclaimed. "You may go."

Kelda had left the Headmistress's study feeling vibrations of disapproval following her and it was with a sigh of relief that she reached the passage outside.

She realised that Mrs. Gladwin disliked her, although she found her useful and she had wondered why until one of the older girls enlightened her,

"Keep out of the dragon's way, Kelda." she had warned. "She is on the warpath and you know that she takes it out on you because you are so pretty."

Kelda had been too surprised to reply, but that evening when she had at last been able to retire to the garret bedroom where she slept, she had looked into the small discoloured mirror that hung on the wall over the ancient chest of drawers.

'Am I really pretty?' she asked herself and knew that it really was the truth.

She had come to Mrs. Gladwin's Seminary for Young Ladies when she was fifteen from the orphanage where she had lived for three years after her father and mother had been killed in an earthquake in Turkey.

Philip Lawrence had been an archaeologist and the National Geographical Society had sent him on a journey of exploration to Turkey. It was a considerable concession that they had allowed him because he had insisted on taking his wife with him.

There had been no question of the Society paying for anyone else, but somehow Philip Lawrence had scraped together the money to take his only child along as well.

It was nothing new for Kelda to accompany her father and mother on their travels and she had loved every moment of it.

When her father and mother had been killed, she had always bitterly regretted that on that particular day she had not been with them.

She had been very tired after a long expedition that they had just taken and they had left her behind in the cheap boarding house where they had stayed the night since she was still asleep when they departed they had not woken her.

Often she would cry not only because she had lost them but also because she had not said 'goodbye' to the two people she loved most and who comprised her whole world.

After that she had never really been able to find out who had decided that she should go to an orphanage on the outskirts of London.

She supposed that it was one of the Missionaries who had taken charge of her, but she had been suffering from shock and nothing had seemed real until she found herself a 'charity child' with some fifty orphans of varying ages, many of them having been in the orphanage since the moment they were born.

They had accepted it philosophically because they had never known anything else, but to Kelda who had been brought up with love and understanding, knowing the companionship of her dear father and the gentle sweetness of her mother and it had been like being plunged into the deepest hell with no chance of escape.

For three years she had suffered the almost intolerable humiliation of finding herself a nonentity, of being ordered about as if she had no feelings, of enduring bad food and little of it and having to sleep with a dozen other children in a ward where they shivered miserably in the winter and panted with heat in the summer.

It had been an inexpressible relief when at fifteen she was told that she must start to earn her own living and was sent to Mrs. Gladwin's Seminary.

Here at least she heard cultured voices and ate what seemed good food even though the pupils often complained about it.

What was more important to Kelda than anything else was that she was now able to pick up her education once again from where, on entering the orphanage, she had been obliged to relinquish it.

Most of the children in the orphanage could neither read nor write and, while a voluntary teacher came in for three hours a day to teach them, there was no provision made for those who were more advanced or, like Kelda, extremely intelligent.

At the Seminary it was easy for her to take a lesson book up to her bedroom at night and, although she was often too tired to absorb all she wished, over the years she had gradually become almost as knowledgeable as her father would have wanted her to be.

The Mistresses were constantly changing, but one or two were kind enough to lend her books of their own and sometimes even to explain to her problems she did not understand.

There was a French mistress, an elderly woman who she carried secret cups of coffee to after she had retired to bed, until she reciprocated by talking to her in French.

"You have a natural Parisian accent, my child," she said, "but you must practise your verbs. The English are always very lazy over their verbs."

Kelda already spoke a certain amount of French, but she had been determined that she would be as fluent as her mother had been.

She therefore waited on the Mademoiselle assiduously and was rewarded eventually by being told,

"Anyone who did not look at you would think that you were French. If they heard you speaking in the dark, they might easily be deceived."

It was a nice compliment that Kelda, who had never received any before, treasured in her heart.

It had been a special delight to her when two years ago Yvette de Villon had come to the school.

She was French and she came, Kelda discovered, from a family that was well-known and respected in France.

Kelda was not supposed to make friends with any of the girls, but only to wait on them by pressing their gowns and mending anything that was beyond their own capabilities.

Kelda had managed by sheer persistence to ingratiate herself with the pretty French girl until Yvette confided in her and talked to her as an equal.

Even so she was afraid to presume too much on their association and she thought now that Yvette, who was often unpredictable, might resent it if she intruded on her grief.

What, Kelda asked herself, could have made Yvette cry?

She was not like some of the other girls who wept if one of the Teachers was angry with them or who when they first arrived were desperately homesick.

Yvette was proud and in consequence had no particular 'bosom friend' in the school to whom she could turn in times of trouble, real or imaginary.

Her weeping, however, sounded so desperate that Kelda could bear it no longer.

She knocked gently on the door and after a moment's silence Yvette's voice, quavering and hesitating, asked,

"W-who – is it?"

Kelda then turned the handle and, because she did not wish to be overheard, replied in a whisper,

"It is me, Kelda."

"Come in."

Kelda slipped into the room.

It was very small, as were all the rooms in the Seminary, but it had a personal look about it because Yvette had so many pretty things of her own in it.

There was an expensive lace cover in the narrow bedstead and a frilly satin cushion on the only chair. The wardrobe door was open and Kelda could see a good profusion of gowns in bright colours all of which had come from expensive Paris dressmakers.

But the face that was turned up towards Kelda was very different from Yvette's usually attractive one.

Her eyes were swollen, her small nose was red and tears were running down her cheeks.

"What is the matter?"

Kelda saw as she spoke that Yvette held a crumpled letter in one hand and the other one clutched a handkerchief sodden with tears.

"Has something happened to someone you love," Kelda asked.

It was what she always suspected whenever she found that anybody was deeply unhappy, remembering how she had felt herself when her father and mother had died so suddenly and there had been nobody she could turn to for comfort.

"No – it is not – that," Yvette stammered.

Kelda knelt down beside her.

"Tell me what has upset you," she said. "Perhaps I can be of help."

"Nobody can – help," Yvette replied, her voice breaking.

"Please, tell me," Kelda begged.

"I have had a letter, a letter – from my uncle."

"And it has upset you?"

"*I hate him*! I have always hated him and now I have to go and live with him."

Kelda remembered that like herself Yvette was an orphan. Nevertheless she had a great number of relations in France. Every holiday when she returned to Paris she had stayed with aunts and uncles who had impressive-sounding titles and romantic Châteaux on the Loire and Villas in the South.

Yvette returned to the school with stories of the exciting times she had had, how many parties she had attended and it seemed very strange now that she should be thrown into such despondency.

Aloud Kelda said,

"I did not know that you hated any of your relatives. Which uncle are you to stay with?"

"My English uncle," Yvette answered. "He is horrible and if I live with him I shall never see France again – and all my friends."

She burst into tears once again and Kelda rose to fetch her a fresh handkerchief from the chest of drawers.

She put it into Yvette's hand and then, as the French girl mopped her eyes, she said,

"I had no idea that you had an English uncle. You have never spoken about him."

"Why should I – tell you? I hate him, but my aunt married him."

"And he lives in England?" Kelda asked. "Well, that will not be too bad. After all you have many friends who are English here at the school."

"He does not live in England," Yvette replied, "but in Senegal."

It took Kelda a second or two to remember where Senegal was and then she thought that she must be mistaken.

"You cannot mean Senegal in West Africa?"

Yvette nodded.

"My uncle lives there because he dislikes Society. He is a recluse – an eccentric. Why should I have to live with someone like that?"

Her voice sounded desperate.

"Is there any – reason why you should – obey him?" Kelda asked her hesitatingly.

"Mama and Papa made him my Guardian a long time before they died," Yvette replied.

She paused for a moment to mop her eyes before she went on,

"Aunt Ginette was alive then and, as she was Mama's younger sister, I suppose that they thought that, if anything should happen to them, Aunt Ginette would take Mama's place. But she is dead and that leaves Uncle Maximus whom I have always hated and who I am sure hates me."

"If that is true, why would he want you to go and live with him?" Kelda then asked her practically.

"I expect he wants to imprison me in Africa where I can never see anybody I am fond of and have no parties or enjoy anything that will amuse me and I will then just become old and embittered as he is."

"How do you know he is like that?" Kelda asked.

"I saw him five years ago," Yvette answered, "and some of my other relatives have seen him since and they say that he has grown even worse than he was then."

Kelda could think of no reply to this and after a moment Yvette went on,

"There is some mystery about him which makes them always stop talking when I come into the room, but I have often heard my cousins say laughingly that I have too much money and might become cynical like Uncle Maximus."

"He is rich then," Kelda said. "Perhaps he wants to leave you all his money."

"I don't want his money," Yvette retorted. "I have plenty of my own. Papa and Mama left me everything they

~9~

had. I may not spend it until I am twenty-one and that is more than three years ahead! Three years when I shall have to live with Uncle Maximus and ask him for every penny I require."

She burst into such a huge flood of tears that Kelda could only put her arms round her and hold her close.

"It may not be as bad as you think," she said soothingly, "and it will be interesting for you to see Senegal."

She remembered her father talking to her about West Africa and claiming that he would like to go there for a visit.

Kelda had been with him once to Algeria, but that had been a long time ago and it was difficult to remember very much about it except that it had been full of sunshine and she and her father and mother had found a great deal that amused them.

They had stayed for a short time in Algiers and found the City fascinating.

"I will look up the geography books about Senegal," she said, "and tell you all about it. Where does your uncle live?"

"I don't care where he lives," Yvette said petulantly. "It will be beastly, like him, and I shall loathe every moment of it!"

"It might be better than you think," Kelda suggested. "Tell me where he lives."

"You can see the address for yourself," Yvette replied and flung the letter she held in her hand onto the floor.

Kelda bent down and picked it up.

She realised that both the envelope and the writing paper were of the thickest and most expensive quality and both bore an impressive crest.

She did not like to make Yvette think that she was prying by reading the letter, but as she looked at the address, noting that it was in Dakar, her eye also caught the first line on the writing paper written in a strong upright hand.

"*My dear niece –* " she read.

It struck her as being an unnecessarily formal manner of addressing Yvette, but aloud she said,

"I am sure there will be much in the books about Dakar and I am certain that it is under French administration. So there will be French people living there and you will not feel as lonely as you anticipate."

"I want to stay in France," Yvette insisted. "I want to be in Paris where I can dance and go to all the lovely balls that are to be given for me when I leave the school at Christmas."

Kelda had thought it likely that, as Yvette would be eighteen at the beginning of next year, she would leave Miss Gladwin's either at Christmas or at Easter.

Because she was fond of the French girl, she had known that she would miss her and at the moment there was no other pupil to take her place in her affections.

"I just don't know what I shall do without you," she observed with a deep sigh.

"If I asked if I could stay here for another six months," Yvette said suddenly, "do you think they would let me?"

Kelda looked down at the letter she still held in her hand.

Somehow she did not know exactly why, but she felt as if there were vibrations of power coming from it and an unmistakable aura of authority.

"I think, if your Guardian says you are to leave, then you will have to do so," she said quietly.

Yvette sprang to her feet.

"Why should I live with someone I hate? Why should he order me about, not even asking me if there is anything else I would prefer to do?"

She paused for a moment before she added angrily,

"I presume you know the answer to that. I would rather live in a garret in Paris than in a Palace in Dakar!"

"Is that what he owns?" Kelda asked curiously.

"I imagine that is what it will be," Yvette replied. "As he is so rich and so pompous, he obviously lords it over the wretched natives."

Kelda put the letter down on the table, resisting an impulse to ask Yvette if she could read it.

'There is really nothing I can do to help her,' she thought sadly.

She was just about to say how sorry she was when there was a knock on the door which made both the girls start.

"Who is it?" Yvette enquired.

"Madam wants to see you in her study, *m'mselle*," one of the maids replied.

She went away without waiting for an answer and they heard her heavy footsteps going down the passage.

Yvette looked at Kelda.

"The dragon will have received a letter as well and I bet she is drooling over it because Uncle Maximus has a title!"

Mrs. Gladwin was a snob who fawned on the parents whose names appeared in *Debrett's Peerage* and it was a joke that never ceased to amuse her pupils.

Yvette was not smiling now.

Instead she carried on,

"You can be sure that the dragon will make me do exactly what Uncle Maximus wants."

"You had better go down the stairs and find out what she has to say," Kelda said, "but you should wash your face first."

"Let her see it as it is," Yvette replied. "I shall try and persuade her to write to my French relatives and protest at my being sent off to some outlandish place, although I doubt if she will do so."

"I think it very unlikely," Kelda agreed, "and even if they do protest, they will not have any authority under the Law."

"Uncle Maximus has not taken any interest in me until now," Yvette wailed. "He has not written to me at Christmas or even sent me a card. Why should he want me to live with him? Why this sudden interest?"

"It does seem strange," Kelda agreed. "Perhaps he feels lonely."

"Lonely? Uncle Maximus? According to Cousin Jacques, recluse though he may be, he always has a mistress."

Kelda looked shocked.

"I cannot believe your cousin told you that!"

"Not exactly," Yvette admitted, "but he visited Uncle Maximus when he was on his way to Cape Town and he told his brother when he did not know that I was listening, that when he called on him, he had a glimpse of a beautiful woman.

"'Mind you.' he added, 'I have a suspicion that she was a *métise*.'"

Yvette wrinkled her brow.

"What is a *métise*? I asked Aunt Jeanne-Marie, but she would not tell me."

Kelda knew it meant the offspring of a white Company employee and a local woman, but she was not going to explain that to Yvette.

Instead she replied,

"I will look it up in the dictionary and let you know."

"I have done that already, but it was not there, unless I had the spelling wrong."

"You must hurry to Madam," Kelda insisted. "You know how cross she gets if one keeps her waiting."

"Why should I care if I am leaving?" Yvette retorted.

Kelda was tidying her hair and then she found her another handkerchief.

"I will wash these," she said, picking up the two tearstained ones. "Is there anything else I can do for you?"

"Nothing, nothing unless you can cast a spell on Uncle Maximus so he will fall dead!"

She walked across the room and, as she reached the door, she stopped.

"That is quite an idea. I believe there is lots of Black Magic in Africa. I shall try to find a witch doctor as soon as I get there and see if he can dispose of my uncle for me!"

Kelda gave a little cry of horror.

"That is a wicked thing to say! I know you will do nothing of the sort."

"Don't be too sure," Yvette answered sharply and flounced down the passage.

Kelda sighed and began automatically to tidy the room. She was sorry for Yvette. At the same time she wished that she had the opportunity of travelling to Senegal or anywhere else in the world as she had done so often when her father had been alive.

She knew now that the one thing that had been harder to bear than anything else was the feeling of being so restricted and restrained first by the drab dark walls of the orphanage and then by the Seminary.

When her father and mother were alive, they had never stayed for long in any one place.

Even if her father had not been sent on an important expedition, he had travelled about England giving lectures at Universities and Kelda could remember twice going to Edinburgh.

Their journeys had seldom been very comfortable, but it had been an excitement to be on the move.

More than anything else it had been a thrill to be in a foreign country, to ride on the back of a camel or a stubborn mule or to sail in a small boat with a large sail up a river to places that could not be reached by any other means.

'Oh, Papa, I miss you,' Kelda said beneath her breath.

She knew that the eight years since he had died had been a nightmare from which she half-believed she might still awake.

To look back made her remember that, while Yvette was not yet eighteen and was going out into the world for the first time, she would be twenty-one in July.

And Kelda supposed that her life would never alter from what it was at the moment.

She often wondered to herself, if she left the Seminary, if she would be able to find other employment of a more congenial nature.

Although she had often considered it, she thought it was unlikely and in a way she clung to Mrs. Gladwin because with her she was with girls who came from cultured families.

It was not that they or Mrs. Gladwin considered her to be their equal. She continually reminded her that she came from an orphanage and was nothing but a 'charity child'.

At first Kelda had resented it, feeling that she must reply that her father was a gentleman and her mother a lady, even if they had very little money.

Then she decided that such retorts only made the situation more difficult than it was at the moment.

Mrs. Gladwin liked humiliating her because unlike the servants she could not leave nor would she answer back as the Governesses could do.

She therefore taught herself to always control her feelings, to try not to listen when Mrs. Gladwin found fault incessantly and expected her to be eternally grateful for having a roof over her head and food to eat.

She was certainly paid little enough for her services a quarter of what any of the servants received but she knew that if she was dissatisfied there was nothing she could do about it.

Even these meagre wages were overdue and, because Kelda loathed having to ask for what she was owed and being told once again how grateful she should be for being where she was, she had not even mentioned the fact to her employer.

She crossed the room to shut the wardrobe door and, as she did so, looking at the gowns hanging inside it, many of which Yvette had only worn two or three times.

Kelda remembered how pretty her mother had always looked, despite the fact that she could never afford anything expensive.

"It is not only what you spend," she had said once, "it is having good taste and knowing what suits one's real self."

'Perhaps if I had the chance,' Kelda thought, 'I too would have good taste.'

She had only to look in the mirror to realise that the grey gown that she wore, which was made of coarse cotton, was unbecoming and appeared, as indeed she was, poverty-stricken.

It was, of course, chosen by Mrs. Gladwin, who ever since she had come to the Seminary had insisted on repeating the same grey garments she had worn in the orphanage rather than buying her dresses of a brighter and more cheerful colour.

"Please, Madam," she had asked a year ago, "as I am having a new gown, could it be in blue or green?"

"I consider both those colours quite unsuitable for your position," Mrs. Gladwin replied acidly. "What is more, they would show the dirt."

"I wash my gowns every week," Kelda countered quickly.

"I should have thought that was unnecessarily often," Mrs. Gladwin replied, determined to find fault. "And the uniform I choose for you is what I permit you to wear and there will be no arguments about it."

She was dismissed and as she left the study Kelda knew that it had been a forlorn hope anyway that she might be allowed to look more attractive.

Now, as she closed the wardrobe door, she thought of what she would buy if she could afford it. She was sure that blue and pale green would be becoming to her, as they had been to her mother.

She had the same fair golden hair, the same large blue-grey eyes that were the colour of the morning mist and her skin was transparently clear, although she was pale and far too thin from overwork.

She caught a glimpse of herself in the mirror and turned away from it.

What was the point of pretending? She would wear grey and the years ahead would be grey too.

If Yvette only knew it, she was very lucky to be able to escape to Senegal or anywhere else in the world.

There were innumerable duties that kept Kelda busy until supper time.

One of the jobs that had been thought up for her by Mrs. Gladwin was that she should wait on the Mistresses who had supper in their own rooms.

They took it in turns to supervise the pupils in the large dining room where everybody had to eat at luncheontime.

The Mistresses insisted that in the evening those who were not on duty should be served in their own sitting room, where they could add to the school fare delicacies that had been purchased either by themselves or sent to them by relatives.

At first Mrs. Gladwin had resisted such an innovation. Then when she found that there were no reasonable arguments she could use against it, she assuaged her pride by saying that the servants were too busy, but that Kelda could wait on the Mistresses, bringing their meals in from the kitchen and washing up afterwards.

Kelda had not really minded for as a result she often enjoyed titbits that the Mistresses left, which was a change from the school meals that were repeated in monotonous rotation from week to week with no variations.

Tonight, when she entered the staff room. it was to find an animated conversation taking place.

"I said to her," Miss Dawson, one of the older Mistresses, was declaiming, "'I have no intention, Madam, of spending my holiday by travelling to some outlandish part of the world. I dislike the sea and always have and I have no plans for ever leaving these shores again'."

There was a burst of laughter as Kelda put the heavy tray down on a side table.

"What did she say to that?"

"She merely dismissed me and sent for Miss Jenkins."

"Did you accept her proposition?" someone asked. "Tell us, Jenky. We are all ears."

"Of course I did not," Miss Jenkins, who was the sporty Games Mistress, replied. "I am spending all my holiday with my fiancé at his home. I would not give that up for a trip to Heaven and back again!"

Again there was laughter as Kelda ladled out the soup and set it down on the table in front of each of the Mistresses.

"Who did she try next?" someone questioned.

"I think she has been through the lot of us," Miss Dawson said. "I know Ashton told me before she went out this evening that she had refused and I think Miss Hart has said 'no'."

"Madam is so keen on pleasing this Nobleman," Miss Jenkins said, "that I cannot think why she does not go herself or alternatively she could send Kelda."

Kelda started at the sound of her own name and they all laughed.

"As a matter of fact," Miss Jenkins said, "I actually did."

"You didn't!" Miss Dawson exclaimed. "You must have been feeling cheeky. We all know what she thinks of Kelda."

"She was furious. That is why I said it," Miss Jenkins laughed. "She knows we are all aware that Kelda is the only one in this place whom she can treat in that highhanded manner, as if she was the great Penjandrum himself. None of us would stick it."

"That is true," Miss Jenkins said. "I have often wondered, Kelda, why you don't leave."

Kelda was bringing the last bowl of soup to the table and she smiled.

"The answer to that is simple," she said. "It is because I have nowhere else to go."

"And no money either, I suppose," Miss Jenkins sniggered.

"I have not been paid for six months," Kelda replied, "and if I was I doubt if it would get me further than Piccadilly Circus."

They all laughed as if she had said something very funny.

"I think it's a crying shame," Miss Jenkins said. "But never mind perhaps one day a rich uncle you've forgotten about will turn up and carry you off to Timbuktu. One never knows one's luck."

"I can always go on hoping," Kelda answered.

She picked up the tray and went out of the room. As she closed the door behind her, she heard Miss Dawson saying,

"It's a disgrace the way Madam treats that nice girl."

"That is what I think," Miss Ashton said, "but there is nothing we can do about it and I suppose as a 'charity child' she is lucky to be here."

Kelda did not wait to hear any more. She hurried down towards the kitchen, feeling as if her feet echoed the same words,

'Charity child! Charity child!'

She felt as if they were branded on her and she would never be anything else however hard she tried. A 'charity child' everyone could trample over and for whom there was little hope now or in the future.

*

When she had finished washing up the Mistresses' supper Kelda made a cup of cocoa and carried it upstairs to Yvette.

It was strictly against the rules, but she thought that it might help the French girl to sleep, knowing that her unhappiness would doubtless keep her tossing and turning all through the night.

She opened the door to find that Yvette was already undressed and sitting in front of the mirror with a sulky expression on her face.

"I have brought you some cocoa," Kelda said.

"That is kind of you, Kelda," Yvette tried to smile. "I could not eat any supper, I was too unhappy."

"Are you hungry? Shall I go downstairs and make you a sandwich?"

"No, I don't want anything to eat, but I will enjoy the cocoa. Did you put plenty of sugar in it?"

"Three teaspoonfuls," Kelda answered. "'Hot and sweet' was what my mother always prescribed when somebody has had a shock."

"It is certainly what I have had."

"What did Madam say to you?"

"Only what you know already that I have to go and live with Uncle Maximus. He has instructed her to send me to him, as if I was a parcel, accompanied by one of the Mistresses from the school to see that I reach him without mishap."

"The Mistresses have all refused to go."

"I know that," Yvette said. "Madam called me into the study after prayers to ask, 'have you any relations in England who would accompany you to Dakar?'"

"'No, Madam,' I replied, 'and if I had, they would not take me. They all dislike my uncle as much as I do.'"

Kelda gave a little laugh.

"I am sure that Madam was shocked at your speaking like that."

"Horrified!" Yvette agreed. "She looked down that long nose of hers and said,

"'That is not the way to speak of your uncle, Yvette. I am sure that what he is doing is in your best interests.'

"'My best interests, Madam,' I replied, 'would be to live in France with the relations I love and who love me. I have no wish to go to Senegal and I have a very good mind to run away!'"

Kelda laughed and it was a sound of pure enjoyment.

"How brave of you! I don't know how you dared to speak to her like that."

Yvette shrugged her shoulders in a typically French gesture.

"She can do nothing to me now that is any worse than what Uncle Maximus is doing."

"What did she say?"

"She gave me a long lecture on propriety and how I should not only damage myself but also the reputation of the school by speaking in such a 'pert and unladylike fashion'."

Yvette deliberately imitated Mrs. Gladwin's voice as she said the last phrase and both she and Kelda laughed again.

"What did she say after that?" Kelda asked.

"She went on until she ran out of breath. Then I said, 'I am not surprised that none of the Mistresses will accompany me to Senegal and I most certainly have no wish to be buried alive there myself. If it is impossible for you to find anybody to accompany me, perhaps you could tell my uncle it would be best for me to stay here. Or, alternatively, let Kelda come with me. She, at least, as an explorer's daughter, will not object to travelling into darkest Africa'."

Kelda gave a gasp.

"That is what Miss Jenkins suggested. What did Madam reply?"

"I did not wait to hear," Yvette answered. "I went out of the room while she was still gasping for breath like a goldfish that has been left out of the water."

"She must have been furious!" Kelda said.

There was a note in her voice that made Yvette say quickly,

"Oh, Kelda, I hope I did not make her so angry that she takes it out on you."

"So do I," Kelda nodded.

She felt apprehensive, thinking that if two people had made the same suggestion it would infuriate Madam to the point where she would think of some unpleasant punishment for her.

She changed the subject as it made her feel rather nervous and asked,

"When do you go?"

"Two days before the end of term. Madam would not let me leave if Uncle Maximus had not insisted that I should travel in some specific ship which stops at Dakar on its way to the Cape."

"It sounds very exciting!" Kelda exclaimed.

"You know how I feel about it," Yvette said in a forlorn voice. "I do wish that you could come with me. At least there would be someone human to talk to. If old Dawson had taken up Madam's proposal, I think I should have died! You know what a bore she is at any time."

"I would love to come with you," Kelda admitted, "but you know as well as I do that it would be like asking for the moon."

"I suppose so," Yvette said despairingly. "But you say all the Mistresses have refused."

"They all said they had at supper," Kelda replied, "including Miss Ashton, who is not in tonight."

"Then who will the dragon send with me?" Yvette asked.

"I have no idea. Perhaps she has a friend who would like to journey to Africa or perhaps she will go herself."

"Then I shall definitely jump overboard," Yvette said firmly. "I am not travelling with old Gladwin and that's a fact!"

Even as she spoke, the door opened and then to Yvette's and Kelda's astonishment Mrs. Gladwin came into the room.

It was unusual for her to leave her own quarters once supper was over and she seldom visited the girls' bedrooms except for her inspection which took place weekly in the morning.

Then she would walk around deliberately to find fault and it was Kelda's self-appointed task to hide away anything that the girls had forgotten that she thought might evoke Mrs. Gladwin's disapproval before she appeared.

Food, fruit and sweets were totally forbidden and anything decorative and in any way ostentatious was always in danger of being confiscated.

As Mrs. Gladwin stepped into the room, it was so unexpected and in a way so unusual that for several perceptible seconds Yvette forgot to rise from her chair.

Mrs. Gladwin was, however, glaring at Kelda.

"I had a suspicion I might find you here, Kelda," she began. "As I have told you before, I will not have you gossiping in the young ladies' rooms, which is neither proper nor in the sphere of your duties. If you have nothing better to do, I will certainly find you something."

"As Mademoiselle was so very upset today," Kelda said in her soft voice, "I brought her something warm to drink, knowing that it was in a way a medication."

"If Yvette needs one, I will send for the physician," Mrs. Gladwin said automatically.

She then looked sharply at Yvette.

"I presume,' she said, "you have been crying again and making a quite unnecessary fuss about your uncle's plans for your future."

As she was already so overwrought, the tears gathered again in Yvette's eyes and Mrs. Gladwin rattled on,

"You must learn to control yourself. As I have told you so often, self-control comes from being civilised and properly educated."

Yvette did not reply and, as she was searching for her handkerchief in the belt of her gown, two tears rolled down her cheeks.

"I have been thinking over the difficulties of your reaching Dakar," Mrs. Gladwin said. "That is why I have come to ask you once again if there is anyone you know in England who would be prepared to accompany you on this journey."

"I have already told you, Madam, I know of no one," Yvette responded.

"There is no Governess you have had in the past who would for a remuneration, a small one, of course, act as your chaperone?"

"The Governess I had before I came here," Yvette replied, "has a good position in Paris teaching the children of the Duc de Beauclaire. So I am quite certain she would be unable to come with me, even if she wanted to, which I very much doubt."

Mrs. Gladwin ignored the last words, which were obviously rude and stood in the centre of the small bedroom thinking.

Kelda would have so liked to inch past her and reach the door, but she had a feeling it would only bring more wrath down upon her head.

She therefore stood where she was, hoping that she could fade into the background and not draw any unnecessary attention to herself.

"Very well," Mrs. Gladwin said, at last as if she had finally made up her mind, "if that is actually the position, the only thing I can do is to send Kelda with you."

She paused for a moment, ignoring the startled expressions on both Yvette's and Kelda's faces and went on,

"Of course being a 'charity child' she is nothing more than a servant and she can act in the capacity of your lady's maid as well as keeping you constantly in her sight."

There was still no response from either of the two girls and she went on as if to herself,

"I shall send a letter at once to the Steamship Company explaining your circumstances and I am quite certain that your uncle's name will carry great weight with them so there will be no difficulty about your having the best possible attention."

She paused before she continued,

"I shall also ask if there are any respectable English people on board. The Steamship authorities will, I believe, as they do in the case of ladies travelling to India, invite one of the lady passengers to keep an eye on you and act as your official chaperone until you do reach Dakar."

Yvette found her voice eventually.

"I shall be – all right with – Kelda."

"That is what I hope, although I am none too confident of her capabilities in looking after herself, let alone you," Mrs. Gladwin retorted. "But I am certain, yes, I am quite certain that there will be someone on board you can be entrusted to once the ship has left Southampton. I shall take you on board myself so that your uncle will have no reason to worry about you."

Mrs. Gladwin stopped speaking to look at Kelda's wide eyes and pale face.

"As for you, Kelda," she insisted, "if you fail the charge I have put upon you, if you are unworthy of my trust, I can assure you that you will never darken the doors of this house ever again!"

Mrs. Gladwin did not wait for any reply, but she merely turned with a rustling of her silk petticoats.

"Go to bed, Yvette and say a prayer of gratitude to God that you have somebody like myself to take care of you, who has your best interests at heart."

Mrs. Gladwin left the room.

For a moment neither Yvette nor Kelda moved.

It was almost as if they had been turned into stone.

Then Kelda, beneath her breath and in a voice that was barely above a whisper, said,

"It is not – true. I could not have – heard what she said. I must be – dreaming."

"It is true," Yvette answered, "although I can hardly believe it! And, Kelda, if anything could make the journey to my uncle bearable, it is knowing that you are coming with me. I shall say a prayer of gratitude all right, but only because without you I know that I should die of misery on the voyage."

CHAPTER TWO

As the Steamship moved out of Southampton Harbour and joined the English Channel, Kelda had gripped her fingers together tightly to make sure that she was not dreaming.

She could hardly believe it was possible that for the moment at any rate she was leaving behind the misery she had felt at the Seminary and in England itself where for the last eight years she had been consistently unhappy to the point of despair.

Now like the wave of a magic wand everything was changed.

At least for two whole months she would be free of Mrs. Gladwin's fault-finding and of continually being reminded that she was nothing but a 'charity child'.

It had been a thrill for her, although not for Yvette, that she was on board a ship.

Because Lord Orsett was obviously very rich and influential, they were allotted two of the best cabins on the First Class deck communicating with each other.

There was a large number of obliging Stewards to carry their luggage and to ask if there was anything they could do to serve them.

Kelda's luggage looked pathetically small beside the large amount of trunks in which she had packed Yvette's gowns, bonnets and sunshades and a whole number of other things she had insisted on buying at the last moment.

"If I do have to go to some benighted hole at the other end of the world," she had said defiantly to Mrs. Gladwin,

"I am not going to be ashamed of my appearance and so until I actually leave I intend to spend the time shopping."

For once Mrs. Gladwin had no viable arguments as to why she should not do so.

Because the Mistresses could not be spared the time, Kelda had accompanied Yvette on a number of shopping expeditions for which a closed carriage was hired, as, of course, Yvette was not allowed to travel by public transport.

It was all so exciting that Kelda had found herself praying at night that nothing would happen to prevent her from going to Senegal, even though she well knew that every day their departure grew nearer, Yvette became more despondent.

"I shall be buried alive," she kept saying over and over again and there was nothing that Kelda could say to console her.

She wrote to all her relatives in Paris begging them to intervene on her behalf, but they wrote back saying that there was nothing they could do as her uncle was her Guardian.

Kelda, who saw all the letters, had a feeling that they were over-awed by Lord Orsett's wealth and standing.

"Why did he go to Senegal in the first place?" she asked.

Yvette shrugged her shoulders.

"I cannot imagine unless it was to be different from everyone else."

"Had he been there before he married your aunt?"

"I don't think so. I have always heard that Aunt Ginette was very pretty and enjoyed gaiety and parties."

"It seems strange that he should have taken her to Africa."

"Everything about Uncle Maximus is so strange," Yvette said, "and I cannot understand why Mama ever made him my Guardian."

"I suppose she thought that he would look after you properly and could afford to do so," Kelda replied.

"You keep talking about his money," Yvette said sharply. "Have you forgotten that I am an heiress?"

"Only now that your father and mother are dead," Kelda pointed out gently.

Yvette did not reply because she hated to talk about her uncle and Kelda knew that she was becoming increasingly apprehensive about seeing him again.

There were so many questions she wanted to ask, but as she knew that they upset Yvette, she thought it best to wait until they had actually begun their journey towards her mysterious relative to live in a part of Africa that seemed mysterious too.

Kelda had searched every guide book in the school to find out something about Senegal, but, although it had been officially a French Colony since 1848, there was very little written about it in the history and travel books, which were predominately English.

The geography books contented themselves with merely showing a map of the area and reiterating that it was under French rule.

She did discover, however, that four years earlier a decree had created the Government of French West Africa headed by a Governor-General.

She found that Senegal had the equivalent of a Council of a French Department, but she was not quite certain what this meant.

She longed to have someone to explain all these queries to her before she actually arrived in Senegal and she thought that this was perhaps where she missed her father's wisdom and knowledge of the world more than she had ever missed him before.

'How thrilled Papa would be to think that I was going exploring again,' she told herself and then wondered desperately how long her exploration would last.

Mrs. Gladwin had been quite firm that she was to return to England as soon as Yvette had settled down with her uncle.

"Get it into your head, Kelda," she had said in her disagreeable voice, "that you are only going as a travelling companion with Mademoiselle since I cannot find anyone else. You will not intrude in any way upon his Lordship's household and you will return at the first possible opportunity."

She paused and added almost spitefully,

"I shall expect you back in January without fail."

Kelda nodded her head in agreement because there was nothing else she could do.

But she knew that once Mrs. Gladwin had left the ship they were travelling in, she would pray every night that she would never see her again and so find some excuse for staying in Dakar or any other part of the world where she could earn her living in a different way.

'Perhaps there will be schools where I could teach or I might even serve in a shop,' she told herself.

Then she laughed as she remembered the native bazaars and markets she had attended with her father and mother and knew that the idea of a white woman being employed in them was very impractical if not impossible.

For the present moment, however, she was in a ship travelling from one Port to another and so in a 'no-man's land' where she was free of any restrictions except those imposed upon her by her own sense of propriety.

Mrs. Gladwin had, of course, written to the Steamship Company seeking a chaperone for Yvette.

The Purser had introduced her to an elderly couple, a Methodist Minister and his wife, who were returning to South Africa after a visit to England to see their children.

As they had little money of their own, they were deeply grateful that their congregation had contrived to raise the money for their fares and had insisted, as they were both elderly, that they should travel First Class.

They had been overwhelmed when Mrs. Gladwin bore down on them like a ship in full sail and hastily agreed to anything she asked them for.

Kelda had realised they were far too retiring and unassuming to think of interfering with anyone, least of all with someone as pretty and obviously aristocratic as Yvette.

Because in her drab garments they took Kelda to be little more than a senior servant, they could talk to her more easily, but after two days at sea when they both felt unwell she found herself looking after them rather than them looking after Yvette and herself.

The first night aboard Yvette began to take an interest in the other passengers.

"A rather dull lot, I think," she confided to Kelda, "with the exception of one young man who looks interesting."

"Where is he?" Kelda asked.

It had been announced the first night at dinner that passengers could sit anywhere they wished and that the places at the Captain's and the Chief Officers' tables would be allotted the following day.

Kelda had travelled often enough to know that this was a precaution on the part of the Captain against overlooking an important passenger who by rights should have been sitting at his table only to find later that there was no place for him.

She thought it wise to ask the Chief Steward when they entered the Dining Saloon if she and Yvette could have one of the small tables for two.

"Why have you asked for this table?" Yvette enquired as soon as they were seated.

"It will give us a chance to look around," Kelda explained, "and know who to avoid."

Yvette laughed.

"I never thought of that, but I can see quite a number of people who will come into that category. My father used to laugh about ships' bores who told the same story over and over again from Portsmouth to Port Said and Mama used to run from the gossips who disparaged anyone who was in the least attractive and said the most slanderous things about them."

Yvette laughed again.

"That will be me!"

"In which case please be careful," Kelda pleaded. "Don't forget that I am in charge of you and if you behave badly I shall get the blame."

"Who is to know how I behave?" Yvette asked her. "Besides, if I have an outrageous reputation by the time I arrive at Dakar perhaps Uncle Maximus will send me home to Paris in disgrace."

"I would not bank on it, but please, dearest Yvette, remember how angry he will be with me and I shall be sent back, not to Paris like you, but to the dreaded Mrs. Gladwin."

Yvette made a grimace.

"Then we must certainly stop that from happening. And I have every intention, Kelda, of keeping you with me whatever Uncle Maximus may say."

This statement did not make Kelda feel as happy as it should have done.

From all she had heard about Lord Orsett, she was quite certain that he would do exactly what he wanted to do and make everyone else do the same.

If he wished her to leave, she would leave whatever Yvette might say in the matter, but she went on praying that someone somehow would save her from returning to England.

Yvette had noticed a rather good-looking young man the first night and Kelda had seen when she pointed him out that he had noticed her.

It might have been chance but Kelda suspected that it was connivance when after they had been allotted places at the Captain's table for luncheon the following day, the young man was seated next to Yvette.

They had learned that his name was Rémy Mendès, but at luncheon they only exchanged commonplace remarks on the weather, the speed of the ship and the fact that there were so few young people on board it looked as if it would be difficult to arrange sports of any kind.

"I shall have to get my exercise by jogging round the deck," Monsieur Mendès said, "but I would much rather play badminton or quoits, although I believe that quoits is rather hard on the hands."

"I can play badminton," Yvette volunteered, "although not very well, I am afraid."

'Then I must certainly challenge you to a game," Monsieur Mendès replied instantly, as she had obviously intended him to do.

As soon as luncheon was over, Yvette and Kelda went to the Saloon as it was too rough and too cold for them to go outside on deck.

Kelda was not at all surprised that they had no sooner seated themselves in one corner of the room and ordered coffee than Monsieur Mendès asked if he could join them.

Yvette introduced Kelda to him and it was obvious that after one glance at her clothes, he thought she was merely a paid chaperone and after a formal bow he concentrated entirely on Yvette.

"Now we can talk," he said in a manner that was obviously intended only for her ears.

His dark eyes looked into Yvette's and there was no doubt about the look of admiration in them or that he was already very attracted to her.

'I wonder if I ought to do anything about it,' Kelda asked herself and had no idea what the answer should be.

"Are you going to Cape Town?" he asked Yvette. "I believe it is a very attractive place, although I have never been there before."

"No, I am going to Dakar," Yvette replied.

"To Dakar?"

There was no doubt that Monsieur Mendès was astonished.

Yvette did not reply and he exclaimed,

"I cannot believe it! Did you really say Dakar?"

"I have to go there to stay with my uncle," Yvette explained, "but I assure you I would much rather be going on to Cape Town."

Kelda thought it was rather indiscreet of her to tell her troubles so quickly to a stranger.

But Monsieur Mendès asserted,

"I would much rather you came to Dakar, because that is where I am going. But I can hardly believe that anyone as lovely as you would set foot in such a benighted place."

"Do you live in Dakar?" Yvette enquired.

"Only temporarily, thank God. I am, as it happens, for the next three months Diplomatic Equerry to the Governor-General."

Yvette clasped her hands together.

"But that is wonderful. I shall see you."

"You can be sure of that," he smiled. "Who is your uncle?"

"Lord Orsett."

Again the astonishment on Monsieur Mendès face was very apparent.

"Lord Orsett? But he never has visitors and I most certainly never suspected that he had a niece who looks like you."

"Tell me about Dakar," Yvette suggested. "As you can well imagine, I have no wish to go there when I might be in Paris."

"I can understand that," Monsieur Mendès said. "I too will very much miss Paris, but thank Goodness I shall be back there in time for the spring."

"There will be chestnut trees blossoming in the *Champs-Élysées*," Yvette said wistfully.

"And pretty flowers in the *Bois de Boulogne*."

"There will be balls and parties," Yvette continued in a rapt voice, "and I had planned how I would dance until dawn."

"That is just what you should do," Monsieur Mendès said. "But how is it possible you are travelling to Dakar?"

"Lord Orsett is my uncle by marriage and also my Guardian."

"I remember hearing that he had had a French wife," Monsieur Mendès said. "I suppose that is originally why he came to live in Dakar, but then she must have hated it as much as you will."

"What shall I do?" Yvette asked him. "Tell me what I should do."

"I promise you one thing. I will do everything in my power to make your stay in Dakar as pleasant as possible."

"But you will be going away."

"Not until the middle of March and a great deal may happen before then."

The way he spoke made Yvette feel shy and she looked down so that her eyelashes were dark against her pale skin.

'She is very pretty,' Kelda thought to herself. 'It is not surprising that he cannot take his eyes from her face.'

She was wondering at the same time what Lord Orsett would say if they arrived in Dakar accompanied by a young man.

It was obvious from that moment that Monsieur Mendès was bowled over by Yvette and she by him.

"He is most charming, delightful and intelligent," Yvette said when she and Kelda were undressing on the first night and on the second she sighed with a dreamy look in her eyes,

"I think, Kelda, I am falling in love!"

"Please, Yvette, please be careful," Kelda begged her. "I am quite sure that it is unwise to be precipitate in such matters. We know nothing about Monsieur Mendès. Your uncle may not approve of him."

"I am quite sure that Uncle Maximus approves only of himself!" Yvette scowled. "But I will find out everything you want to know. Monsieur Mendès has asked me to meet him on the top deck tomorrow morning and, if it is not raining, we can sit somewhere sheltered and talk without being watched by those old pussycats who were staring at us at dinner tonight."

It was obvious, Kelda thought, that the elderly women at the Captain's table should look with raised eyebrows at the way that Yvette and Monsieur Mendès were engrossed with each other all through the meal.

He made no effort to speak to the lady on his other side and, as Yvette had Kelda next to her, she saw no point in dividing her attention.

Kelda had therefore been left to talk to an elderly trader who she learned had often visited Senegal to buy groundnuts, which were, he now informed her, their only appreciable export at the moment.

He was partly deaf and, although Kelda would have liked to ask him about Senegal, she found it somewhat embarrassing when she had to shout every question several times before he understood her.

After dinner was over to Kelda's consternation, Yvette and Monsieur Mendès suddenly disappeared.

She could not ask anyone if they had seen them and, although she wandered restlessly from lounge to lounge there was no sign of them and after a while she gave up the search and retired to her own cabin.

She was certain that Mrs. Gladwin would disapprove, but she told herself philosophically that 'what the eye did not see, the heart did not grieve over'.

Nevertheless, when after midnight Yvette came to bed, she remonstrated with her.

"You might have told me where you were going," she began reproachfully.

"I did not know myself. Monsieur Mendès whisked me away to the writing room where nobody ever goes."

"I never thought of looking in there," Kelda admitted.

"We were hiding from you too," Yvette said mischievously.

"You know that you should do nothing of the sort," Kelda remonstrated with her, but in a mild tone because she was quite certain that Yvette would not listen to her whatever she said.

"I am enjoying myself," Yvette said, sitting down on the side of Kelda's bed and looking exquisitely lovely in a gown of coral pink with tulle of the same colour framing her white shoulders.

"You are worrying me," Kelda answered.

"There is no need to worry," Yvette replied, "and quite frankly I am beginning to enjoy the voyage and even the thought of being in Dakar, at least for the next three months, is not so upsetting."

"Suppose your uncle will not let you see Monsieur Mendès once you have arrived?"

"I know what you are trying to say, Kelda, but then I have found out everything about him and I can assure you that he is very respectable."

"Well, that is a relief at any rate."

"His father is a member of the Chamber of Deputies and Rémy has decided to become a Politician. His family is not aristocratic as the members of the old *régime*, like my great aunts are, but they are well known and rich."

Yvette paused for a moment to add,

"At least Uncle Maximus cannot say he is a fortune-hunter."

Kelda sat up in bed.

"Yvette, you are not thinking of marrying him?"

"He has not asked me yet," Yvette replied, "but he will. He says he is in love with me and he is also impressed by who I am. I can further his Political ambitions if nothing else."

"And you think that is important to him?"

"Not if he is really in love with me and he will be. Make no mistake about that, Kelda. He will be."

Kelda thought rather helplessly that she knew nothing about love.

She was well aware from the confidences Yvette had made to her that she had already flirted with quite a succession of young men when she had been on her holidays in Paris. She had a feeling, however, that this was something more serious.

Then she told herself that she was being absurd.

Shipboard romances were notoriously fleeting and doubtless when they did reach Dakar Yvette would already be bored with Monsieur Mendès and be looking out for another man.

The book she had been reading before she went to bed had told Kelda that there were practically no white women in Dakar, in which case she had thought that Yvette would have the choice of many men who would be only too thrilled to see anything so attractive from the world they had left behind.

"Rémy Mendès is gaining experience," Yvette was saying, "which his father thinks will be of great use to him when he too becomes a Deputy."

"So that is why he is going to Dakar?"

"Yes. As he told me, as Diplomatic Equerry to the Governor and he has already held the same position in Algiers."

Kelda thought eagerly that she would have liked to talk to him about Algiers, since she had been there, but realised that as things were Monsieur Mendès would have no wish to talk to her when he might be talking to Yvette.

"Of course my aunts in Paris were talking about my making a brilliant alliance with one of the great families of France. They were even thinking of the young Duc de Féneon."

"If that is true," Kelda remarked, "then you must not involve yourself too closely with Monsieur Mendès."

"So if I am to live with Uncle Maximus," Yvette said, as if she was working it out for herself, "I am not likely to come into contact with the Duc or anyone else."

"I just cannot believe that your uncle wishes to tie you down in Dakar for ever," Kelda objected. "Perhaps he too is thinking of your future and so wishes to see you and talk to you about it."

She was well aware that French families made arranged marriages, especially when a girl was as rich and as well-born as Yvette.

It was something she thought of as unpleasant, almost barbaric, but she had never said so to Yvette, not wishing to upset her and knowing that as far as she herself was concerned there would be no chance of marriage either arranged or otherwise.

She felt, however, that in the circumstances she ought to prevent Yvette from falling in love with a young man who had not been approved of by her relations, but how she could do that she had no idea.

The following day and the day after she found herself either sitting alone in the Saloon or on deck unless she sought the company of the Methodist Minister and his wife.

It was quite obvious that none of the other passengers considered her important enough even to bother to make her acquaintance.

This, Kelda knew, was due to her clothes.

She had brought with her only the grey cotton gowns that she had been made to wear at the Seminary and as a rare concession to the cold Mrs. Gladwin had provided her with a thick black wool cape that covered her completely.

On her head she was made to wear the same black straw bonnet that had been modelled on those she had worn at the orphanage. It was exceedingly unbecoming, hiding her face and tied under her chin with cheap black ribbons.

Black gloves and sensible elastic-sided boots completed her ensemble and everything else she possessed went into one small bag that was so shabby even the porters and Stewards looked at it with disdain.

Kelda wasted no time being sorry for herself as she had no idea that she had anything to be sorry about.

She could hear the sea, she could feel the wind and indeed she knew with an irrepressible gladness that they were steaming towards the sunshine.

She felt as if she had been cold with the constriction in her heart from the moment her father and mother had died until now when she was escaping from the prisons that she had been incarcerated in.

She was intelligent enough to know too that, having for the first time for eight years not only enough to eat, but a choice of food contributed to this new feeling of happiness.

It was also an inexpressible luxury not to have to rise at five o'clock in the morning as she had done both in the orphanage and at the Seminary.

"I shall get fat," she told Yvette, "if I do so little and eat so much. It is something I have not been able to do for years.'

"Well, I feel as if I never want to eat anything again," Yvette replied, "and that is another reason why I think I must be in love."

By the time they were through the Bay of Biscay and moving down the West coast of North Africa, Yvette was no longer *thinking* that she was in love.

It was obvious that she was from the brightness of her eyes and the radiance that seemed to emanate from her whenever she and Rémy Mendès were together.

Kelda gave up begging her to be careful and not to display her affections too obviously. It was a waste of words and she knew when Yvette came into her bedroom at one o'clock in the morning what had happened.

"I am engaged, Kelda! And Rémy and I are going to be married in Paris at Easter!"

Kelda gave a little gasp.

"But supposing Lord Orsett will not allow you to marry each other?"

"Why should he stop me?" Yvette asked her. "I intend to be the wife of the future Prime Minister of France and even Uncle Maximus must be a little impressed by that."

"Suppose he is angry because you have made such an important decision without asking him first? He may not approve of Monsieur Mendès."

"Rémy says that he will follow in the footsteps of his father, who is very important in the Political world and, now we have talked things over, I find that he is very much richer than I thought he was. We will have a house in Paris and a Château on his father's estate, which is enormous. Oh, Kelda, I am so happy."

She spoke in an ecstatic tone that made Kelda's arms go out towards her.

"I am so glad, dearest, I am really," she said. "It is just that I think I am as frightened of your uncle as you are."

"I am not frightened of Uncle Maximus anymore now. Rémy says he will look after and protect me and love me for the rest of our lives. What more can I want?"

"What indeed," Kelda agreed.

At the same time she was worried.

Everything she had heard about Lord Orsett made her feel that he was not going to like decisions made without his approval, especially one that meant his niece would be staying with him for a very short time.

"We shall go to Paris at the beginning of the year," Yvette was saying, "because I intend to have a magnificent trousseau and that exercise, as you know, takes time."

"We?" Kelda questioned.

"You are coming with me," Yvette said. "You know I could not do without you and you will love Paris as I do."

"What will your relations say?"

"We don't have to be concerned with my relations anymore," Yvette replied sweepingly, "only with Rémy and Rémy is very grateful to you for the tactful way you have behaved."

*

The next day, after Yvette had been with Rémy all the morning, she came bursting into Kelda's room just before luncheon.

"Rémy has an idea," she enthused, "and I think it is very sensible."

"What is it?" Kelda asked putting down the book she had been reading.

"It is that you should change your appearance!"

"Change my appearance?" Kelda repeated stupidly.

"I told Rémy who you are," Yvette went on, "and he is sure he has heard of your father. Anyway he is very impressed that he had lectured to the Geographical Society, which is very highly thought of in France."

Kelda then wondered curiously what was coming next.

"Rémy is appalled," Yvette continued, "at the horrible way you have been treated by Mrs. Gladwin and the clothes you have been made to wear. He says that we will need your support and help in facing Uncle Maximus, so you must look like someone of high standing whose opinion will carry weight."

"How can I do that?" Kelda asked, not understanding what Yvette was trying to tell her. "He says that men like Uncle Maximus are tremendously impressed by appearances. He has made the suggestion, and I should have thought of it before, that I should dress you in my clothes to look like the lady you are."

"B-but I could – not do that," Kelda said quickly and without thinking.

"Why not?" Yvette asked.

"Because they are your clothes — they belong to you — and so what would Mrs. Gladwin say?"

Yvette laughed.

"Mrs. Gladwin is hundreds of miles away and personally I could not care what she says. I have heaps of dresses with me and Rémy is right, Uncle Maximus must look upon you as an equal otherwise he is not going to listen to anything you have to say."

"I doubt if he will listen to me anyway," Kelda said humbly.

"It is important that he should do so, at least Rémy thinks so. After all I have been sent out to Dakar in your charge."

"Even if I do look different," Kelda said after a moment, "do you not suppose that Mrs. Gladwin has told him exactly who I am and what position I occupy in her school?"

"I am sure she has done," Yvette said with a mischievous smile, "and you will remember that as we were leaving she gave me a letter to take to Uncle Maximus. It is a pity that he will never receive it!"

"W-what — do you mean?"

"I am going to tear it up this moment and throw the pieces out of my porthole."

"You cannot do that!" Kelda exclaimed. "It is a personal letter."

"I am sure it is full of lies, but neither of us will ever know for certain because I am not going to read it and I will not let you read it either. It would only make you feel miserable."

She went from the cabin as she spoke and Kelda heard her rummaging about in the next cabin.

"I have found it!" she cried after a moment.

There was the sound of tearing paper and then she came back into Kelda's cabin with a waste-paper basket in her hand.

"I am not going to open my porthole tonight, but it is all in here in minute pieces, which I am going to throw into the sea at first light. Then no one will ever know, not even the fish, what the dragon wrote about you."

Kelda looked at her wide-eyed.

"I am sure it is – wrong."

"On the contrary, it is right," Yvette contradicted, "and, as Rémy thinks it is right, there is no argument about it. You are *free*, Kelda, free of that horrible old woman and everything that has happened in the past since your father and mother died."

"I-I cannot believe it," Kelda sighed and she felt the tears coming into her eyes.

Yvette suddenly threw her arms around her and kissed her.

"I love you, Kelda," she said, "and, if I am starting a new life, then so are you. We are all going to be very happy. I am going to bed now and tomorrow we are going to start planning my trousseau. I want to look lovely, absolutely lovely for Rémy."

*

The following morning, as Kelda got out of bed wearing the stiff harsh calico nightgown that had been provided for her by Mrs. Gladwin, Yvette came into her cabin.

"I thought I heard you moving about," she said. "I have been too excited to sleep and so I have been sorting out a whole lot of things that you can wear until we can buy some more."

"I am sure I ought not to take them," Kelda protested, but Yvette did not listen to her.

She brought in from her cabin a whole pile of gowns, underclothes, nightgowns, so many that Kelda could only gasp and find it hard to express her thanks.

"You must not give me all — those!" she expostulated.

"I have enough for my immediate needs," Yvette answered, "and actually I wrote to my cousin in Paris, who always helps me choose my gowns, and told her to send me as quickly as possible a whole mass of dresses which I shall need in Dakar."

"But you brought dozens from London," Kelda exclaimed.

"London clothes are not as smart as anything that comes from Paris," she replied. "But what a good thing from your point of view that I bought so much."

That was certainly true, Kelda thought and she sorted out what Yvette had given her and could hardly believe that after all these years she was actually to look what she described to herself as 'a human being'.

She and Yvette were the same height, but Kelda was very much thinner and she sat down at once taking in the gowns at the waist.

Yvette had, as was fashionable, a small waist, much pinched in, but Kelda's was smaller still and entirely natural.

Although Yvette had insisted that she should have a pair of her beautifully made French corsets, there was really no need for them because after years of work and running up and down innumerable stairs dozens of times a day and having so little to eat, there was not a spare ounce of flesh on Kelda's body.

Only the fact that she was very young and perfectly made ensured that the curves of her breasts were very feminine and, although she was unaware of it, when she was naked she did look like a statue of a Greek Goddess.

When she was finally all dressed up in Yvette's lace-trimmed underclothes, wearing silk stockings for the first time in her life and a gown that had cost an astronomical sum in the *Rue de la Paix*, she thought that she would be too shy ever to leave her cabin.

"I really cannot go out like this," she said to Yvette in a kind of panic. "What will people think?"

"What people?" Yvette asked. "I doubt if those old fossils outside will even notice you. But you look very attractive, dearest Kelda, and, if Rémy prefers you to me, I swear I will kill you!"

Kelda laughed.

"I think it is very unlikely, but – Yvette, I don't know how to – thank you."

Her voice broke on the words and the tears started to run down her cheeks.

It was not only the clothes that were so lovely, it was that after being treated as a 'charity child' and being crushed for so long the transformation did something for her very spirit and she felt as if she was a phoenix rising from the ashes of herself.

Yvette hugged her.

"If you cry, you will then spoil the whole effect and I want Rémy to be stunned by your appearance. After all it was his idea. Let's go now and show him right away. He is waiting for me."

Feeling shyer than she had ever felt before, Kelda followed Yvette from their cabin to the forward lounge where Rémy Mendès was waiting for them.

As she entered the room, she saw his eyes widen for a moment in astonishment.

Then he threw out his hands to cry,

"*C'est magnifique*! I congratulate you, Yvette. It is exactly how I want her to be."

"You are – both so – kind," Kelda murmured, finding it hard to speak.

"Sit down," Rémy Mendès suggested. "We are going to celebrate two things, first of all, Mademoiselle Lawrence, we are going to drink to the future of Yvette and myself. Then we are going to drink to yours and I have a feeling that it is going to be very different from what you thought it might be when you came aboard."

"If it is," Kelda said, "it is entirely thanks to you, *monsieur*."

"I shall certainly take the credit," he smiled, "when your marriage follows ours."

Yvette clapped her hands together.

"You are so clever. Of course, when we do go to Paris, we shall find dearest Kelda a delightful husband, someone very distinguished and very rich."

"Just like me!" Rémy said with a twinkle in his eye.

"There could not be anyone quite as wonderful as you," Yvette added.

"I don't want you to think of me," Kelda said in a low voice, "but you know what I think about you."

They had forgotten for a moment that Kelda was there and she thought when she raised her glass of champagne to them, that she had never seen two people look so happy.

"It is just like a Fairytale," she said to Yvette later that evening when she was dressing for dinner in an evening gown that she thought was as beautiful as Titania herself might have worn on a Midsummer's night.

"Of course it is," Yvette agreed, "and Rémy is my Prince Charming and I am not only his Princess but your Fairy Godmother!"

"I could certainly go to a ball in this gown," Kelda murmured.

"But you will, of course, you will. When we go to Paris, there will be a ball every night. Rémy loves dancing just as I do and he says his father will give the most spectacular ball that Paris has ever seen when we announce our engagement."

There were so many things to plan and, as they steamed down the coast of Africa, Yvette was busy when she was not with Rémy making lists of everything she wanted to buy in Paris.

"You cannot want twenty sunshades!" Kelda expostulated.

"I hardly think twenty will be enough," Yvette replied. "After all one with each summer ensemble and, don't forget, it will be summer almost as soon as we are married."

Only when she was alone did Kelda find herself worrying about Lord Orsett.

He did not now seem to be as terrifying as he had done when they first boarded the ship at Southampton, when Kelda in despair had been crying every night as she remembered Mrs. Gladwin reiterating over and over again that she was to come straight home as soon as his Lordship had no further need of her services.

At the same time, when she thought about it seriously, Kelda could not help feeling that Lord Orsett might easily take the attitude that Yvette was too young to know her own mind.

She seemed, Kelda thought, older than most girls of her age because of the very social life she had led in Paris and also because she was intelligent

In actual years she was not quite eighteen and she had the uncomfortable feeling that it would matter more to Lord Orsett than anything else.

She was quite certain that he would not be the type of person who would dig deeply into somebody's character but would judge them entirely superficially.

That she thought, was exactly what Rémy Mendès thought about him, although he was too tactful to say so. Otherwise he would not have been so insistent that she should change her appearance.

But she was deeply grateful to him for having done so.

Now she need no longer pull her hair into a tight bun at the back of her head as Mrs. Gladwin had made her do, but could arrange it fashionably so it looked soft and feminine and she knew that then she looked more like her mother.

For the first time since she had found herself alone in the world, she felt unrestricted as if she could behave as she wished to.

Always before she had been forced into acting the part of a 'charity child' who must not show she was better bred or better taught than the other children around her or a servant in a Seminary who must always remember to respect those who felt themselves superior to her.

Now that she could talk as an equal with Rémy Mendès and Yvette, she felt as if the years of misery had rolled away like a cloud and now she was just her father's and mother's daughter.

It was as if she was travelling with them on an expedition, which was an adventure that was filled with laughter and gaiety because they were all together.

Every night, when she said her prayers, she said one of gratitude for Yvette's friendship and for what she knew was a God-given chance of escape.

'Please, God, let it go on happening,' she prayed. 'Don't let Lord Orsett spoil everything by sending me back to England before I have a chance to find anything else to do. And – please – if it is possible – let me go to Paris with Yvette – please – *please* – '

It was a cry that came from her very soul because it was almost impossible to have any real confidence in this newfound happiness that had come to her so unexpectedly like sun on a dark day.

Because she knew that she would always be eternally grateful to Yvette, she prayed for her too.

'She is in love,' she told God. 'Let her and Rémy always love each other – please, God – and make Lord Orsett allow them to marry soon.'

It was a prayer that she said not only in her cabin at night but whenever she saw them together.

There was no doubt now that their love had grown until it was difficult for either of them to see anyone else except each other.

There was an admiration in Rémy's eyes when he looked at Yvette that could not have been anything but sincere and Yvette loved him in a manner that told Kelda, who knew her so well, that her emotion was not just a part of her heart but of her very soul.

'They are so very lucky,' she told herself, 'they have found what everyone in the world seeks which is the other part of themselves and nothing and nobody must ever separate them.'

She felt as she spoke, almost as if she was Joan of Arc with her sword in her hand ready to do battle for what was right and what was true.

As the idea flashed through her mind, she knew that, if it had to be a battle or a crusade, she was already completely and absolutely dedicated to fight it.

CHAPTER THREE

The ship steamed into the Port of Dakar in the early afternoon.

It was very hot, but there was a soft touch of the trade winds to keep the waves dancing and to sweep away the oppression and humidity of the heat.

To Kelda the golden sunshine made her feel as if it seeped into her body, melting away the last of the cold and awakening a new vitality inside her.

Now that the moment had come when they must leave the ship, she felt as if she could not bear to say 'goodbye'.

She wanted it all to go on for ever, steaming away to an unknown horizon, and the fact that her whole life and outlook seemed to have changed since she came aboard made her feel as if she must say 'farewell' to a place that had given her the security of a home.

Also, because they were nearing the moment when Yvette must meet her Guardian, she knew that they were all apprehensive and more than a little nervous.

Although Yvette put a brave face on it and said that she was no longer afraid because she was with Rémy, Kelda knew perceptively that Rémy was feeling anvious too.

There was no doubt that he had much to offer to the woman he would marry. At the same time, knowing how snobby the French aristocrats were, Kelda was sure that the de Villons would not think him Yvette's equal in blood.

The real question was what would Lord Orsett think?

For her it was so exciting to be in Africa and have the chance of visiting a country that she had never seen before that Kelda kept on wishing over and over again that her father was with her.

The coast they were sailing along seemed flatter and lower than she had expected, but standing on deck she had been able to see shores of golden sand with coconut trees growing down to the beach.

As they neared Dakar, she could see, as the City jutted out into the Atlantic, that there were a number of houses with trees clustering protectively around them.

The Captain of the ship had told them when they were nearing Dakar that it had a natural deep-water Port.

He had spoken too of the Island of Gorée, which lay within only a mile off the coast, but which he said bore the curse of the slave trade that had made it wealthy.

Kelda had shivered as he spoke for she had read of the horrors of slavery and the misery of those who were captured and sold suffered when, battened down in the holds of ships, they were carried all over the world.

She tried not think of their sufferings, but to concentrate on looking at Dakar as the ship edged its way slowly into Port.

Yvette and Rémy came up to join her as she stood at the rail looking at the crowds below them.

"There is his Lordship's carriage waiting for you," Rémy declared in a low voice.

He pointed and Kelda and Yvette saw a very smart open carriage drawn by two horses with a white cotton fringed awning to keep off the sun.

There was a coachman wearing an elaborate livery which seemed somehow out of place in the heat and a footman attired in the same way was standing with the crowds staring up at the ship, as if trying to identify those he had come to meet.

"Is my uncle with them?" Yvette asked warily.

"I cannot see him," Rémy replied, "and it would be unlike him to meet a ship himself whoever he was expecting as a guest."

His words brought back to Kelda the fact that Lord Orsett was said to be a recluse and she had the uncomfortable feeling that he was already reaching out towards them, spoiling the light-hearted enjoyment with which they had spent the last week of the voyage.

She had been happy and full of laughter because she felt so different.

Every time she put on one of Yvette's beautiful gowns she felt as if it transformed not only her appearance but also her character and her personality.

Now she no longer suppressed the intelligent things she wanted to say and now she could laugh without being afraid of receiving a rebuke and, most of all, she had a new confidence in herself.

Because Yvette was so kind, she no longer felt afraid all of the time of what tomorrow would bring or of losing her job.

She was ashamed of herself for having been so weak and humble for so long. But she had been menaced by the fact that Mrs. Gladwin could, if she so wished, throw her into the street without a reference and without any money to save her from starving.

It was easy to say that the knowledge that she was very intelligent should have made her believe that she would find work somewhere, but who then would want a 'charity child' with nothing to recommend her except for what she could say about herself?

Now everything was changed, Yvette was her friend and she was dressed as her mother would have liked to see her and, unless all their plans were reversed, Yvette and Rémy would look after her and she would no longer be completely alone in the world.

"You are – both so – kind," she had said last night when once again they had all toasted their future.

There had been tears in her voice and Rémy had smiled at her.

"We want to be kind to you, Kelda," he said, "and I shall always be grateful to you for all you have done for my future wife."

"You know I love you," Yvette had said, "and, when we reach Paris, Rémy has a plan for you. He is sure that one of his three sisters would love you to teach her children English."

Kelda had, with difficulty, restrained her tears.

"It is like – coming into the – sunshine," she said, "after being enveloped in a – fog for years and years."

"That is just what your future will be," Rémy replied. "But don't forget that tomorrow you have to meet Lord Orsett."

There was silence for a moment while all three were thinking what this might mean to them.

"Will you come with us to his house?" Yvette asked Rémy. "If you would, meeting him would not seem so frightening."

"I am sure that would be a mistake," Rémy replied. "He would think I was presuming. I will call formally the day after you arrive. I think it would be unwise for you to tell him that we are engaged until I have asked his permission to pay my addresses to you."

"I will do whatever you say," Yvette replied.

She had spoken in a low voice and Kelda could see that her eyes were troubled.

Now, as the ship came nearer to the quay, Yvette hung frantically on to Rémy's arm.

"We had better go below and get ready to go ashore," Kelda said, "and don't forget we have to thank the kind old people who have looked after us on the voyage."

"We will thank them for not doing so," Yvette replied irrepressibly.

Nevertheless she made a pretty little speech, which delighted the Minister and his wife.

Then, after an impassioned farewell to Rémy, she and Kelda waited in their cabins until there was a knock on the door.

When they pulled it open, there was an elderly man outside very correctly dressed, who explained that he had come on behalf of Lord Orsett to escort them ashore and would collect their luggage after they had left in the carriage for his Lordship's mansion.

They started off down the gangway, Yvette looking over her shoulder as she went for a last glimpse of Rémy. Then the crowds moved aside for them to walk to the carriage.

After the elderly man had helped them into it, the footman jumped up on the box and the horses started off and he stood bare-headed until they had departed.

Now, as they drove down the tree-bordered streets, Kelda had her first chance to look at the people and realised that they were very different from those she had seen when she was in Algiers.

The very first thing she noticed was the kaleidoscope of colour shown in the voluminous *boubous* of the native women. In brilliant blues, purples, greens and pinks, they swept along the roadside looking like huge flowers, their heads swathed in colourful turbans and their feet bare, but their wrists weighed down with jingling bangles.

If the women were impressive, Kelda thought that the men were surely magnificent.

Very tall, they had the broadest shoulders she had ever seen, tapering down to narrow hips and they walked with an athletic grace that again was different from any native she had seen in other parts of the world.

'Papa would be able to tell me about them and of their different tribes,' she mused.

She wondered if Lord Orsett, when she met him, would answer the questions she longed to ask.

They drove in silence for quite some way until the houses were left behind and they were now moving along what seemed nothing but a dusty track with the sea on their left.

The land rose until there were steep cliffs down to the water's edge.

It was then suddenly that Kelda saw in front of them what she thought at first must be a Mosque or some civic building.

It was surrounded by trees except for the side that looked out towards the sea and, when the road ended with large wrought-iron gates tipped with gold, she knew at once that they had reached what Yvette had called her uncle's 'Palace'.

It certainly looked like one, dazzlingly white and sublime in the sunshine.

It was almost like a Georgian house back in England, except that its long windows and its ornamentation gave it an undoubted Eastern look.

There was a flag flying over the pillared portico that Kelda suspected was Lord Orsett's personal standard and, as they swept up to the entrance, she saw that the hibiscus shrubs with their brilliant crimson blossoms made it almost appear as if the big white building was being consumed by fire.

"It is certainly very lovely," she exclaimed.

"I am – frightened," Yvette murmured.

"I am sure there is no need to be," Kelda replied, although she was far from feeling as confident as her words sounded. "Your uncle certainly appreciates beauty if nothing else."

She knew that Yvette wanted to say that this was not particularly comforting, but at that moment the carriage drew up beside a flight of steps covered with a red carpet.

Servants wearing all white, on the front of which was embellished Lord Orsett's Coat of Arms in red, appeared in the doorway.

Yvette climbed out of the carriage slowly and Kelda followed her.

She could not help feeling thankful that she was not wearing those ugly clothes in which Mrs. Gladwin had expected her to appear.

Instead she had chosen for her arrival a pale green gown of Yvette's that made her look very young and spring-like.

The hat she wore was decorated with white roses and green leaves that were the colour of the gown and she thought that she made a perfect foil for Yvette who was in pink in which Rémy liked her better than in any other colour.

It was a very elaborate gown, almost too elaborate, Kelda thought, but she just knew that Yvette wanted to appear at her best, and not only was her hat decorated with roses, but they also appeared on the small sunshade she carried which boasted a handle of pink quartz.

"You look lovely, dearest," Kelda had told Yvette and she thought that Lord Orsett must be made of stone if he did not appreciate how pretty and attractive his niece was.

A servant, who was obviously in command of the rest, invited them in French to follow him and took them through an impressive hall.

As in most large houses in tropical parts of the world there were doors at each end of it, which were left wide open so that what wind there was, could blow to cool the building even at the hottest part of the day.

Through the other door Kelda could see the deep blue of the sea and she knew that Lord Orsett's house, high on the cliffs, would have a special view that she would greatly enjoy.

But for the moment she was too apprehensive of what he himself would be like to be interested in anything else.

A servant opened the door to the left of them and, as he did so, Kelda saw what seemed to be an enormous room with six long windows opening out onto a terrace.

The sun-blinds were half down to keep out the sun and the room itself was dim and cool so that for the moment it was hard to see if it was occupied until at the far end she saw a man rise to his feet and knew at one that it was Lord Orsett.

Yvette walked ahead of her, then as Kelda followed, she saw Lord Orsett for the first time and found him very different from what she had imagined.

To begin with, from the way Yvette always spoke of him, she thought he must be a man of at least fifty or more, but instead he was much younger and had a physique that could rival any of the natives she had admired as they drove from the Port.

Broad-shouldered and dressed in a white suit, he seemed large and overpowering. Then, as she looked at his face, she was startled.

His features were clean-cut and he looked very handsome in an aristocratic and typically English manner. At the same time he also appeared cynical and stern to the point of grimness.

He was looking at Yvette and Kelda thought with a little shiver that he appeared to be inspecting her almost dispassionately without a vestige of affection.

It was a most critical appraisement, she thought, and there was something unnatural and almost unpleasant about it.

"Welcome to Dakar, Yvette," Lord Orsett said in a deep voice that somehow contrived to be cold and impersonal. "I hope you had a pleasant voyage."

Yvette curtseyed.

"Very pleasant, thank you, Uncle Maximus. May I present my friend, Kelda Lawrence, who has accompanied me on the voyage?"

Lord Orsett turned his attention to Kelda, who also curtseyed and found it hard to meet his eyes, although she forced herself to do so.

"Friend?" he queried. "I instructed the woman who runs your school to send a Mistress with you."

"They all refused to come so far as – Africa."

There was a little pause before Yvette said the last word and Kelda knew that she was about to add 'such an outlandish place' but checked herself at the last moment.

"But Miss Lawrence was more obliging," Lord Orsett remarked.

He did not make it sound very complimentary and Kelda commented,

"It has been a privilege, my Lord."

"Kelda is very used to travelling, Uncle Maximus," Yvette said quickly as if she was conscious of his disapproval. "Her father was Philip Lawrence, the archaeologist, and she visited many places with him before he died."

"Indeed."

Lord Orsett did not sound interested and both girls were conscious of his disapproval that Yvette was not accompanied by an older woman than Kelda.

"I must offer you some refreshment," he suggested. "It is hot at this time of the day and most people make it an excuse for a *siesta*."

He spoke as if this was a weakness to which he would not succumb, but before Yvette or Kelda could say anything more, the door then opened and servants came in carrying a tray on which were long cool drinks and small sweetmeats to eat, which Kelda found delicious.

They sat down on the sofas and chairs, which were so large and comfortable that Kelda was certain that Lord Orsett must have chosen them himself.

She took a quick glance around the room and then decided if he loved beauty outside his house, he most certainly enjoyed both beauty and comfort in it. The room was furnished in exquisite taste with pictures on the walls that she was sure were exceptional and what was unusual was that the room was uncluttered, unlike what she knew was fashionable in most houses in England.

There were some fine pieces of china and carvings that she was certain had been done by native craftsmen, but otherwise the room with its very fine proportions had a cool emptiness, which she knew, as her father had told her, was characteristic of the great architects who had built beautiful houses in the eighteenth century.

However it was difficult to think of anything except their host.

He sat back at his ease, but it would have been impossible to ignore him, Kelda thought, because his very personality seemed to exude strength and power.

And something else that made her afraid.

She tried to analyse what it was and thought it might be a kind of domination of will, as if he was so determined to have his own way that one felt drawn to him irresistibly as if by a magnet.

"What do you think of him?" Yvette asked her a little later when they had been shown to their bedrooms.

"I think he is exceedingly frightening," Kelda replied, before she had time to consider her words.

"So you know how I am feeling," Yvette said. "How can I tell him, how can I possibly tell him, Kelda, that I am engaged to Rémy?"

"I should say nothing," Kelda advised, "until Rémy calls on you tomorrow."

"I am sure that is wise," Yvette agreed with a little sigh. "I feel if we argue with him he would crush us as if we were insects beneath his foot."

That, Kelda thought, was true, but that it would be wise not to say so.

She suddenly felt that both she and Yvette were somehow small and very insignificant.

Here they were in Africa and, unless Lord Orsett agreed to what they wished, they were to all intents and purposes now prisoners in this magnificent mansion and there was no one to whom they could appeal for help or even advice.

Then she decided that she was frightening herself unnecessarily and on no account must Yvette know what she was thinking.

Instead she walked over to the window to look out at what she had known would be an exquisitely beautiful view.

The Atlantic, glorious and blue as the Madonna's robe, lay in front of her ending in a misty horizon where the sea met the sky.

To the left she could just see the island of Gorée and to the right the coastline stretched away, golden with sand and green with coconut trees.

The fishermen were putting out to sea in little pointed boats, which she had read were called *pirogues*. There was something delicate and romantic about them and she wondered if she would ever have the chance to go in one.

Behind her sitting on the bed which looked as large and luxurious as the rest of the room, Yvette was talking.

Kelda turned from the window.

"You did not tell me," she said, "that your uncle was so young. I expected a much older man, at least old enough to be your father."

"He seems very old to me."

"How old is he?"

"I think about thirty-six or thirty-seven," Yvette replied, "and that is old enough in all conscience."

Kelda smiled.

"He would not be flattered to hear you say so."

"I don't suppose that he would care what I thought or said about him," Yvette replied petulantly. "You can easily see what he is like, completely engrossed in himself and his own consequence. Rémy says that he is not liked by any of the young men in Dakar because he condescends to them, but he is a good friend of the Governor-General."

"1 expects he condescends to him too," Kelda replied. "I do wonder why he should stay here when he is English. After all, it is a French Colony."

"I suppose as my aunt was French he prefers the French to the English. Some people do, you know."

Yvette was teasing Kelda because she had often laughed at her for being so patriotic and proud of her own country.

"What have the English ever done for you," she asked once, "except shove you into an orphanage?"

"Whatever they do or do not do, I am still English," Kelda replied.

"And I am French, thank Heaven!" Yvette had parried proudly.

"We should walk about with our flags sewn on us," Kelda said.

And both laughed.

Now, thinking of Lord Orsett she felt that as an Englishman he should be living in his own country.

'Surely he has houses and large estates in England if he is as rich as they say he is,' she thought. "Why should he want to spend his money in Dakar?"

It was indeed a mystery and she thought that she was never likely to get an answer to her question.

"Do you suppose we ought to go downstairs and talk to Uncle Maximus?" Yvette asked.

"It would be polite," Kelda answered. "I would like to see the rest of the house and if it is cool enough perhaps we could sit out on the terrace and look at the sea."

"I hate the sea!" Yvette replied. "I want to look out of a window and see all the roofs of Paris. I want my Rémy to take me dancing. I want to hear the conversation and the gossip of people who enjoy life, which, as you can see for yourself, is something that Uncle Maximus does not do."

"Then why does he stay here?" Kelda asked again.

"Only he can answer that question, but I doubt if you would get a truthful answer out of him."

"Let's go down and try," Kelda suggested.

They went down the stairs and when they reached the hall the head servant told them that he had been instructed by his Lordship to show them any part of the house they wished to see. Then there would be tea waiting for them on the terrace.

It was a relief that they would be able to look at everything without being accompanied by their host and, as they went from one huge beautiful room to another, Kelda knew that she had been right in thinking that Lord Orsett had exceptionally good taste.

He had managed to combine things he had brought from Europe with those that he had either collected or had made for him in Senegal.

There were carvings that she would like to be able to talk to someone knowledgeable about, knowing that they were very old and doubtless steeped in the legends of Africa.

There were metals that she thought must be very precious and weaving that had a special charm of its own.

There were many things she wanted to stop and view, but she saw that Yvette was bored and she told herself that there would be plenty of time later.

They hurried on and finally found themselves on the terrace with an almost English tea waiting for them served by several servants.

"Do you think Uncle Maximus ever entertains people here?" Yvette asked. "There is plenty of room to do so."

"It was you who told me that he was a recluse," Kelda replied.

"That is what they said in Paris and Rémy told me that, with the one exception that he sometimes dines with the Governor-General, he never appears to go anywhere."

"What does he do all the time?"

Yvette shrugged her shoulders.

"Perhaps he just sits hating everybody or practising some special magic of his own."

Kelda did not reply and after a moment Yvette said,

"You have not forgotten that I want to use black magic on him. But I have a feeling that it would have to be very strong and very potent."

"Let us hope you will get everything you want without resorting to such tactics," Kelda replied.

At the same time she thought that Lord Orsett was a very mysterious man.

Because the house was so big, she had a feeling that she and Yvette were isolated in it, even while she told herself that it was ridiculous to think such a thing.

There was no sign of Lord Orsett after they had finished their tea, when the head servant appeared again to tell them that their luggage had arrived and was being unpacked and that dinner would be at eight o'clock.

Yvette merely nodded to show that she understood what she had been told, but Kelda asked,

"Where shall we meet his Lordship before dinner?"

"I will be waiting, *m'mselle*, at the foot of the stairs to escort you to whichever room his Lordship wishes to receive you in."

"Thank you," Kelda murmured.

She rose to her feet as she spoke and she and Yvette went upstairs.

Because it was early in the year darkness came swiftly and by five o'clock it was already much cooler than it had been all day.

They had celebrated Christmas Day at sea and, while the staff on the Steamship had done their best to make it a joyous festive occasion and there had been crackers to pull and small souvenirs brought in by 'Father Christmas' for all the guests, the passengers had been mostly too old or too dull to make it really amusing.

Kelda, however, had enjoyed it all although Yvette and Rémy had been too interested in each other to want to take part.

They had not listened to the concert that had taken place in the lounge, although they had danced to the band that had played later in the evening.

Now in the sunshine of Dakar it was difficult to think that in England there would still frost, snow, ice and hail storms and that, if she was at the Seminary, she would be shivering at night in the garret in which she slept because Mrs. Gladwin would never provide her with enough blankets.

Upstairs they found two maids in each room unpacking their gowns.

They were both pretty girls dressed in cotton gowns such as housemaids would wear in England, but with their heads swathed in red turbans to match the large red insignia worn by the men servants.

"His Lordship undoubtedly likes colours," Kelda remarked when she and Yvette were alone and the maids had withdrawn.

"Why should you say that?" Yvette asked.

"His servants are so colourful and there is lots of colour in the rooms, although they give the impression of being all white."

"What are you suggesting that we should do about it?" Yvette asked. "Paint our faces the colours of the rainbow?"

"No, not that," Kelda smiled, "but do wear one of your brighter gowns this evening. You know we have to make a good impression on him."

"I will wear the cherry-coloured tulle that Rémy likes."

"In which case I will wear the blue chiffon you gave me."

"Do you think that is smart enough for his Lordship?" Yvette teased her.

"You are the important person," Kelda answered, "and personally I do admire myself so much in the lovely clothes you have given me that it does not worry me what his Lordship thinks one way or the other."

"I wish I could say the same."

Yvette gave a little groan and added,

"Just you think, Kelda, if I had not met Rémy, how miserable I should be feeling at this moment. Supposing I thought I had to be shut up here for years and years with no one to talk to except Uncle Maximus ?"

"There must be Europeans living in Dakar."

"Only men and according to Rémy, Uncle Maximus never asks anyone to his house who is young. Rémy has only been here twice when he accompanied the Governor-General for some reason or other."

Kelda did not reply, but she could understand what Yvette was saying and she thought that anyone so full of life and energy would doubtless find it extremely dull after she had known the gaieties and fun of Paris.

When she was dressed for dinner and stood for a moment at the window looking at the moonlight touching the waves and turning them to silver and the sky was filled with stars that twinkled like diamonds in the darkness, she wished that she at any rate could stay in Dakar for a long time.

To her the alternative was not Paris and parties, it was humiliation and hard work in the Seminary.

As she thought about it, she said a little prayer of gratitude, because whatever happened in the future, for the moment everything was different from what it had been for eight long miserable years.

They went down the stairs and the servant who was waiting took them down a wide cool corridor to a room that they had not previously visited when they had toured the house.

It had long windows that overlooked both the sea and the land, although it was too dark to see anything outside.

As it happened, Kelda only had eyes for the room itself. Unlike the rest of the house, large though it was, it was filled with books on every wall and books were also stacked on tables and even on the floor.

"I thought perhaps you would like to see my special Sanctum where I spend most of my time," Lord Orsett said to Yvette, "so I have invited you here this evening, although I doubt if you will have many invitations to join me here in the future."

"Why is that?" Yvette enquired.

"Because this is where I work."

"What sort of work?"

"I am writing a history of the West African tribes."

Kelda made an involuntary sound of excitement and Lord Orsett turned towards her.

"That surprises you, Miss Lawrence?"

"I am really interested, my Lord. When I saw the carvings you have, I longed to know all about them and I felt certain that they had a long history, just as I am sure that the legends of West Africa are fascinating."

Lord Orsett looked surprised and then he said almost sharply to Yvette,

"And are you as interested, Yvette, as your friend?"

"I am more interested in the present than the past," Yvette replied. "If I have to, I would rather study the great history of Paris than anywhere else."

She spoke provocatively and Lord Orsett frowned.

Kelda knew that Yvette had annoyed him and he said abruptly,

"I thought perhaps you would like a glass of wine before dinner and, as you have such a *penchant* for Paris, it is perhaps appropriate that I can offer you a glass of champagne."

"Thank you," Yvette said. "When were you last in Paris, Uncle Maximus?"

"A long time ago and it is a City that I have no intention of ever returning to."

There was no disguising the contemptuous way he spoke.

"How can you say something like that?" Yvette exclaimed. "Paris is the most wonderful and the most exciting City in the world."

"I presume you have seen a great many others to compare it with?" Lord Orsett sneered.

"Enough to know what I like and where I want to live," Yvette answered.

Her uncle did not reply and, watching him, Kelda thought that his eyes were suddenly steel-like and his lips had tightened into a hard line.

'Yvette is antagonising him,' she thought and, as she was determined to be conciliatory, she asked,

"Are all your books in here about Africa?"

"Most of them," Lord Orsett agreed.

"Then I hope you will allow me to read some of them that will tell me what I want to know, otherwise I might bore you by asking too many questions."

"Most of the books are written in French," he replied in an uncompromising voice.

"I can read French quite competently," Kelda pointed out.

She thought by his expression that he did not believe her, but he replied politely,

"In which case I can certainly find you some literature on subjects about which you are particularly curious."

It was a relief when dinner was announced and they went into the large room in which it would have been easy to entertain fifty or even a hundred people without being overcrowded.

The meal was original and really delicious and, as Kelda was afraid that Yvette might antagonise her uncle even further than she had already, she put herself out to ask about the food.

He told her the names of the local fish and she learnt that small cherry tomatoes were one of the favourite products of the district.

It was a conversation that interested her, but she knew by her expression and the manner in which she made no effort to join in, that Yvette was bored.

In fact when they moved after dinner was over into a Reception room that they had seen before, she yawned several times and Kelda wondered if it would be wise to suggest that they should retire to bed.

With a glass of brandy in his hand Lord Orsett sat down beside her and, when there was silence for a moment, Kelda felt instinctively that he was going to say something important.

"You must have wondered, Yvette," he said after a moment, "why I ordered you to come out here to me when I was well aware that you were expecting to go to Paris to live with your French uncles and aunts."

"I thought it was very strange, Uncle Maximus," Yvette replied, "and quite frankly I was upset."

"That is what I expected," Lord Orsett said, "but now I am going to explain to you why I wanted you in Dakar."

He looked at her as he spoke and it was, Kelda felt, as if once again he was appraising her as a man might look at a horse, noting her points and her appearance from her shining dark hair to her small exquisitely shod feet.

"The truth is, Yvette," he then said, "that I have brought you here to be married."

"Married?"

The word was hardly audible as Yvette spoke and yet to Kelda it sounded like a cry that echoed and re-echoed round the room.

"Yes, married," Lord Orsett repeated, "and let me explain why."

He sat back a little more comfortably in his chair and Kelda thought he was well aware that both her eyes and Yvette's were fixed on him with an almost terrified attention.

"I have been living here for some years and I have become extremely interested in the special problem of French colonisation in Senegal, which is different from any other part of their Empire."

He paused as if he expected one or other of them to speak and, when they did not do so, he continued,

"Senegal is now France's major base in West Africa and it is here that her Imperialism will prove most successful."

"What has this to do with me?" Yvette managed to ask.

"That is what I will tell you in due course," Lord Orsett replied. "I have discussed the French ambitions for Senegal with the present Governor-General, who is a very intelligent man and with a number of Officials who have come here from France in the last two years. What they think is wanted more than anything else at the moment is a staple white Society, both in Dakar and St. Louis."

He looked at Kelda as he asked,

"You seem to have an interest in West Africa, so I presume that you are aware of the difficulties that have occurred amongst those administering the country owing to the absence of European women?"

"I can understand that being a – problem," Kelda answered. "At the same time I am not aware of any of the details."

"Then let me inform you of the position to date. Inevitably the French who settled here either for a long or a short term took African mistresses and wives."

Yvette gave a little gasp as if she was feeling shocked, but she did not speak and Lord Orsett went on,

"The wives, *signares* as they are called, of European husbands in a Trading Post, have a certain social status as consorts."

"I think I read about that somewhere," Kelda said, feeling that she was expected to say something.

"A soldier or Company employee sometimes sets his *signare* up in business to augment his own salary and, if he leaves the post indefinitely, his business and property are left to her and her children."

"That seems fair," Kelda murmured.

She was talking because she felt that, if she held Lord Orsett's attention, he would not notice that Yvette had gone very pale and was clenching her fingers tightly together until the knuckles were white.

"The French have decided that this position is not particularly satisfactory," Lord Orsett went on. "As they wish to develop Dakar as an important Port, it is obvious that European women must be persuaded to live here and their presence will have a marked effect on the character of local Society."

"I can – understand that," Kelda said in a low voice.

"At the moment there are considerably fewer than a hundred white women in the whole of Dakar. This is why the French intend to make every possible effort to put pressure on traders and employees of the Government to bring their wives here so that they can persuade other women to join their husbands overseas."

He paused but, as Kelda did not speak, he continued,

"There will be plenty for them to do and the Governor-General himself is determined to set an example, which he is sure will be followed by a number of other Officials."

There was silence until Kelda asked in a voice little above a whisper,

"How – how does he – intend to do – that?"

"The Governor-General was widowed some years ago and intends to marry again," Lord Orsett answered.

He turned his head to look at Yvette.

"I have given him my permission to pay his addresses to you, Yvette, and he will call on you tomorrow morning."

Yvette was obviously paralysed into immobility, but Kelda spoke for her.

"The Governor-General? But surely he is an – old man?"

"He is certainly somewhere between fifty and sixty years of age, but he is young at heart, healthy and most athletic and my niece will have a position not only of importance but one in which she can set an example that I know will have a resounding effect throughout the whole of France."

"Are you really expecting me to marry – an old man and live in this ghastly – uncivilised place?" Yvette asked.

She was so shocked that the words seemed almost to splutter out from her lips and were barely coherent.

"You will take a different view of Dakar when you have lived here for some time," Lord Orsett replied, "and I really assure you that many women would welcome the opportunity of marrying such a distinguished man."

"Then let them have him!" Yvette cried and now her voice was hysterical. "I have no intention of marrying the

Governor-General or of staying in Dakar and you cannot make me do so."

She had risen as she spoke and now she faced her uncle defiantly with her whole body quivering with the intensity of her feelings.

"I think you are mistaken about that," Lord Orsett said in a quiet voice. "I can and will make you do what I wish you to do. While I am your Guardian you are completely dependent on me until you come of age."

"If you think because of that you can force me into a marriage – to a man I have never seen, a man who is old enough to be my father, you are very much mistaken."

Yvette drew a deep breath and added,

"As it happens I was going to tell you tomorrow that I am engaged to Monsieur Rémy Mendès and I will marry no one – no one else but him."

Yvette's voice rang out and, as if the mere mention of Rémy's name gave her courage, she faced Lord Orsett defiantly and the colour came back into her cheeks.

"And who is this Rémy Mendès?" Lord Orsett enquired.

"As it happens he is Diplomatic Equerry to your precious Governor-General and when you meet him, you will understand that he is a very suitable husband for me and not a man with one foot in the grave."

"It is for me to decide whether or not he is suitable," Lord Orsett retorted in a lofty tone. "Where did you meet him?"

"Coming here on the ship."

"A shipboard romance? That is easily forgotten."

Lord Orsett spoke sneeringly and Kelda thought it was what she might have expected.

"That is where you are mistaken," Yvette parried, "I love Rémy with all my heart and he loves me."

"You are persuaded that your quite considerable fortune has nothing to do with it?"

"That is the sort of thing you would think," Yvette declared rudely. "Rémy's father is an extremely rich man. He is also a member of the Chamber of Deputies. He will show you his credentials tomorrow. Then you can see for yourself what he is like."

"He need not waste his time," Lord Orsett stated.

"What do you mean by that?" Yvette asked.

"I mean, to put it bluntly, that I have no intention of having my plans disrupted in any way. You will marry the Governor-General as I order you to do and we will have no more nonsense about impecunious suitors who, if your companion had been doing her job properly, she would not have been allowed him to approach you in the first place."

"You really think you can force this ridiculous idea on me," Yvette demanded furiously.

"I am quite sure I can," Lord Orsett replied. "I have brought you here to be married and married you will be within the next three weeks. And make no mistake, if this unimportant Frenchman tries to communicate with you tomorrow or at any time while you are a guest in my house, I will deal with him in a manner that he will bitterly regret for the rest of his life."

Yvette lost her temper.

"*How dare you!* How dare you threaten me, a citizen of France! You have no right in this country in the first place and you are both mad and bad, as everybody has said you are. If you think you can order me around as if I was a native servant, you are very much mistaken."

She stamped her foot as she finished,

"I hate you, Uncle Maximus! I have always hated you. I would drown myself rather than let you do anything that you have just suggested."

As she spoke, almost screaming the last words at him, Yvette then turned and ran from the room.

She left the door open and Kelda could hear her feet running down the corridor.

She rose and, as she would have followed Yvette, Lord Orsett, who was still lying back comfortably in his chair, asked her,

"Have you nothing to say, Miss Lawrence?"

Kelda knew that he was speaking provocatively.

She turned round to look at him, her eyes very large in her small face.

"If you want the truth, my Lord, I think that what you have suggested is diabolical! It is flying in the face of nature for any man, however important socially, to play at being God."

Lord Orsett did not reply.

He only glared at her and Kelda glared back at him.

Without another word she turned around and left the room, also leaving the door open behind her.

CHAPTER FOUR

As Kelda went slowly up the stairs holding on to the banisters, she realised that she was trembling and her heart was thumping in her breast.

She felt as if she, as well as Yvette, had passed through a traumatic experience that had left her both shaken and shocked.

It just seemed to be inconceivable that Lord Orsett could have thought out anything quite so horrible, indeed as she had said 'diabolical', for someone as charming and sweet as Yvette.

The fact that he had obviously not given any thought to his niece as a person but merely as a puppet to implement his plans made it so much worse.

Everything Yvette had said about him seemed to Kelda to be an understatement of what he was really like.

By the time she had reached the top of the stairs and turned along the corridor towards her bedroom, Kelda was thinking frantically not only of what she would now say to Yvette but what they could do.

As she had expected, Yvette was lying face downwards on her bed, sobbing her heart out.

She sat down on the bed beside her and Yvette turned to fling her arms around Kelda saying as she did so,

"Save me Kelda, *oh, save me*! You know I have to marry Rémy."

"Yes, I know," Kelda said, "and that is why you must stop crying and we must try to see what we can do to circumvent your uncle's wickedness."

She spoke so positively that Yvette's tears stopped suddenly and she looked at Kelda questioningly.

"You really mean you will help me?" she asked, a sob in her voice that was infinitely pathetic.

"Of course I will help you," Kelda said determinedly, "but we have to be clever about this. Remember where we are and how powerful your uncle is."

Yvette took her arms from around Kelda's neck and sat back against the pillows.

"I have never seen you like this before."

"Like what?" Kelda asked her absent-mindedly.

"So strong and brave. I have always thought you were weak because you let yourself be bullied by Mrs. Gladwin."

"But now I am fighting not for myself but for you," Kelda answered, "and that is a very different thing."

"And you think that you will be able to help me?"

There was a desperation behind the question that Kelda was well aware of.

"You know without my saying so that it is not going to be easy," she replied, "but there is Rémy and the first thing we must do is to get in touch with him."

"But how? How?" Yvette asked. "You know Uncle Maximus is going to insult him and you can be quite certain that he will not allow him to write to me let alone see me."

"I have thought of that already," Kelda said. "I cannot believe that Rémy will submit tamely to losing you and you will not only have to be courageous about this but clever and subtle as well."

"How – can I?" Yvette asked. "Tell me – what to do."

Kelda was silent for a moment, her eyes staring at the carving on the bedhead but not seeing it.

Instead she saw the radiance on Rémy's face and on Yvette's that had been there when they looked at each other on board the ship and she had known that this was love as she had always thought it must be like if it was real and came from both the heart and the soul.

'I must save them both,' she thought.

She felt a violent fiery anger rise within her at the thought of what Lord Orsett was trying to do.

"Tell me what you are thinking?" Yvette asked in a frightened voice.

"I was thinking," Kelda replied after a moment, "that if you are to marry Rémy, he will have to take you away from here. And quickly."

"Do you think he can do that?"

"He will have to otherwise your uncle will force you into marriage with the Governor-General."

Yvette gave a little cry of sheer horror.

"To marry anyone other than Rémy would make me want to kill myself," she said. "Even to speak of marriage with an old man makes my flesh creep and I feel – as if I might be sick."

"I can understand that," Kelda said gently. "At the same time we have to realise that you are under the jurisdiction of your Guardian and Rémy is under the Governor-General."

"It is only a temporary appointment."

"I do know that," Kelda answered, "but we are in Dakar and the Governor-General, who is all-powerful, could have him put in prison or sent summarily to France and there would be nothing we could do about it."

She saw the stricken look in Yvette's eyes and added swiftly,

"That is why the first thing we have to do is, I am quite sure, to deceive your uncle into believing that you will do what he wants."

"Do what – he wants?"

Yvette's voice almost rose to a scream.

"You must pretend to agree to his plans," Kelda said. "If he thinks you are fighting him and opposing him, he will watch everything you do and there will be no chance whatsoever of escaping his surveillance."

Yvette realised that what she was saying was sensible and her eyes were fixed on Kelda as she urged her almost beneath her breath,

"Go on."

"We must make plans rapidly and I think the first thing must be for you to apologise to your uncle for your outburst and say that you were taken by surprise, but you are prepared to consider what he suggests. The next step will be to receive the Governor-General when he calls tomorrow."

"Do you think that Uncle Maximus will be hoodwinked into thinking that I will obey him?"

"It depends on how well you act the part," Kelda said. "What we must not do is to make the Governor-General antagonistic towards Rémy."

"No, no of course not."

"I may be wrong," Kelda went on, "but I have a feeling that when he reaches The Palace he will learn, if not from the Governor-General himself, then from the other Equerries and *aides-de-camp* what is being planned for you.

I cannot believe that they are not aware of what the Governor-General and your uncle have in mind for the Colony."

"What will Rémy think when he knows it is intended that I shall marry someone else?"

The question was pathetic and Kelda answered her firmly,

"I do believe that he will be as shocked as you are and he also will be determined to do something about it."

"He loves me! I *know* he loves me," Yvette cried.

"I too am sure of that," Kelda said, "and somehow he will get in touch with us, however difficult it may be."

"Uncle Maximus will – prevent it."

"Rémy will be aware that he will try to do so."

Yvette wiped away the last remaining tears from her eyes.

"Tell me what I am to do," she pleaded. "Tell me exactly so that I shall not make any mistakes."

*

It was a pale and subdued Yvette who walked demurely down the stairs beside Kelda the following morning.

They had learned from the servants that breakfast would be served on the terrace and, as they went to where the meal was laid out under a red striped awning, Lord Orsett rose at their approach.

He was wearing smart riding breeches with a well-tied stock around his neck and the white linen coat he had obviously been wearing was thrown over an adjacent chair.

He looked strong and masculine and, as Kelda had expected, very overpowering.

His eyes were on Yvette as she advanced towards him and, when she reached him, he began,

"Good morning, Yvette. I trust you slept well."

"Quite well, thank you, Uncle Maximus, and I would like to apologise for being so rude last night. You took me by surprise and I was frightened. I hope you will forgive me."

Her words and her conciliatory tone, Kelda could see, took Lord Orsett by surprise.

For a moment he raised his eyebrows.

Then he said,

"Perhaps I was somewhat precipitate on your first evening and, as you have made me an apology, I hope you will accept mine."

"Of course, Uncle Maximus, and it is far too lovely a day to quarrel with anyone."

"That was what we both should think and tomorrow I shall be delighted if you and Miss Lawrence will come riding with me. It is always most pleasant early in the morning before it grows too hot."

"That would be delightful," Kelda interposed. "I so want to see the wild land outside the town, which I am told is very beautiful."

"It is indeed," Lord Orsett nodded.

As they seated themselves at the table, he said as if he suddenly remembered he should enquire after Kelda's wellbeing,

"I hope you too, Miss Lawrence, spent a good night."

"I slept well, my Lord, because, like Yvette, I was tired after being at sea for so long and may I say that I find the waves more attractive when they are murmuring in the distance than when they are rolling beneath me."

Lord Orsett smiled.

"Are you telling me that you were seasick?"

"Surprisingly neither of us suffered from that unfortunate complaint," Kelda replied, "but it was very uncomfortable in the Bay of Biscay."

"That is what I always find," he replied.

The servants brought breakfast and Yvette made a brave attempt to eat.

When they were alone again, Lord Orsett informed them,

"I have received a message from The Palace to say that the Governor-General will call on us at noon. I hope you will assist me to greet him."

"Of course, Uncle Maximus."

Yvette spoke quite naturally and then she said,

"Uncle Maximus, it will make me feel shy if when we meet and before we are even acquainted, you speak of more intimate matters."

As if he was relieved that she was being so pliable, Lord Orsett said swiftly,

"Naturally, I understand, and this will just be a friendly call for you and His Excellency to meet each other. He is an interesting and extremely intelligent man and I feel sure that you will have many tastes in common."

"Does he come from Paris?" Yvette asked.

"He was not born there, but I believe he has lived there for some years of his life. He has also held important posts in other French Provinces besides that of Senegal."

"I shall look forward to hearing about them," Yvette said.

She was acting so well that Kelda had to resist an impulse to clap what was an extremely convincing performance.

It had taken a long time, in fact half the night, for her and Yvette to work out exactly what she should do and what she should say.

It was not only because Yvette was intelligent but also because she loved Rémy so passionately that she was prepared to make every possible effort to do what Kelda suggested.

Kelda was aware now as they went on talking, that Lord Orsett was agreeably surprised at the way Yvette was behaving and was undoubtedly beginning to believe that the scene last night was just the result of shock that he should not have caused in the first place.

As Kelda had said to Yvette last night,

"We know one thing that will be helpful and that is that your uncle has had very little to do with women since your aunt died."

"What about the one my cousin saw when she was here?"

"I don't think that she could have been of any great importance."

"Do you think she was one of the women he talked about last night?"

"I have no idea," Kelda replied, "but anyway it is obvious that she is not here now and I cannot believe that, if you are prepared to be contrite and ready to please him, that he will not be completely deceived."

This, she was quite certain, was what was now happening and while she recognised that there were little discrepancies in what Yvette said that might indeed have made a man more knowledgeable in the ways of women suspicious, she was indeed very sure that Lord Orsett was absolutely deceived.

"What would you like to do now?" he asked when breakfast was over.

Yvette looked at Kelda who already had another idea that she thought was significant.

"If it would not be any trouble," she said, "Yvette and I would love to drive around the town. Actually there are one or two things we would like to buy sometime, not particularly today, but when it is convenient."

She thought for a moment that Lord Orsett gave her a sharp look and then he said,

"Perhaps you would care to drive with me in my new curricle, which has recently been delivered from France. It is, I am told, what dashing young Frenchmen who fancy themselves with the reins, use when they drive in the *Bois de Boulogne*."

Kelda saw Yvette stiffen as he spoke of Paris and, as she was afraid she might betray her longing for the City that meant so much to her, Kelda said quickly,

"That would be lovely. There is so much I want to see of this beautiful country."

She thought for a moment that Lord Orsett looked at her with approval.

Then, as if Yvette felt that it was expected of her, she observed,

"I would enjoy it too, Uncle Maximus, and I am sure that you will have fine horses. I think I remember Mama saying how fond you were of riding."

"You are quite right, Yvette," Lord Orsett said. "I have managed to find myself some excellent horseflesh, as you will see when you both ride with me tomorrow. You have riding habits with you, of course?"

"Of course," Kelda replied, hoping as she spoke that Yvette had two in her trunk.

As they went up the stairs, to make themselves ready, Kelda put her arm around Yvette's waist and whispered in her ear,

"You were absolutely splendid!"

"I felt like throwing a plate at his head," Yvette answered her bitterly.

"Yes, I know. So did I," Kelda agreed. "But you realise that at least we shall be outside the house and there may be an opportunity for Rémy to get in touch with you."

Yvette gave a deep sigh and then asked,

"Supposing he thinks it is hopeless and does not try to communicate with me?"

"He will, if it is at all possible. I am much more afraid that he will do something stupid like challenging your uncle to a duel!"

Yvett's eyes sparkled for a moment at the idea and then she answered,

"You forget that Rémy is a Diplomat and is well aware that he must not do anything that would cause an international incident."

They put on the hats that matched their gowns and Yvette lent Kelda a sunshade and then they went downstairs to find Lord Orsett waiting for them in the hall.

The new curricle drawn by two horses was large enough to accommodate three people in comfort and a groom sat up behind.

They then drove out of the wrought-iron gates with Lord Orsett handling his horses with an expertise that Kelda was sure was exceptional,

She knew that Yvette was looking about her curiously and was aware it was in the hope that by some miracle she might have a chance of seeing Rémy.

As they descended from the high ground and had a glimpse of white sandy beaches and a profusion of flowering shrubs and coconut trees growing down to the sea, Kelda exclaimed effusively at the beauty of what she saw.

This was partly to prevent Lord Orsett from noticing that Yvette had nothing enthusiastic or complimentary to say and because she herself was genuinely entranced by the loveliness of Dakar.

There were only a very few large civic buildings in the town, but there was a number that were nearly completed and it was obvious that the squares, like the roads leading to them, had been planned with the intention of their being decorative.

There were trees in bloom and flowers that made patches of colour against the white buildings.

Because Kelda was so attentive, Lord Orsett pointed out to her the *Palais de Justice* after which he explained to her the plans that were being made to extend the town considerably.

They saw the flower vendors who held up their wares as they passed the market and had an original way of balancing a number of their bouquets in their turbans.

"What a charming idea," Kelda exclaimed.

"It is something so unique to Dakar," Lord Orsett explained, "and I often wonder who thought of it first."

"She should have a statue erected to her memory," Kelda suggested and he replied,

"There are plenty of men who feel that they should go down to posterity in such a way first."

"But even here in Africa you think women are important," Kelda said challengingly.

She thought for a moment that there was a faint smile at the corner of his firm lips as if he realised that she was being deliberately provocative.

"I am sure that women are important everywhere in the world."

It was an evasion and at the same time Kelda felt that she had forced him to consider what he should reply and she felt that in some way she had scored a point over him.

When they had later returned to the house, Kelda thanked him profusely for the drive and Yvette echoed it saying,

"It was very interesting, Uncle Maximus, and I do hope that we can go driving with you again tomorrow."

"I hope you will not be too tired after we have been riding," he replied.

They walked up the long flight of steps into the hall and he drew his gold watch from his waist-coat pocket.

Glancing at it, he suggested,

"You will wish to tidy yourselves or perhaps change before His Excellency arrives."

"Yes, of course, Uncle Maximus. Where shall we find you when we come downstairs?"

"A servant will tell you where I will be," he replied and walked away in the direction of his special study.

Yvette and Kelda went up the stairs in silence. Only when they reached their own rooms did Yvette say almost frantically,

"What am I to say to the Governor-General? Supposing he tells Rémy that I have agreed to marry him?"

"I don't believe that he will ask you to do so in a point-blank manner the first time you meet," Kelda replied. "I may be wrong, and you know far more about Frenchmen than I do, but to me it would seem rather gauche and definitely impolite."

"You are right. He will merely pay me compliments and insinuate a great many things which I can pretend not to understand."

Kelda thought for a moment.

"Look young and innocent, even rather stupid if you like," she said. "That is what he will expect anyway from somebody of your age and, even if he should suggest it, don't be alone with him."

"No, of course not. You must not leave me. You promise you will not leave me."

"I promise," Kelda answered. "But I am sure that His Excellency will behave in a very civilised manner so there is no need for you to feel intimidated."

"If only I could see – Rémy," Yvette murmured. "How can I learn what he is thinking or feeling at this moment? Suppose he thinks I shall give in to Uncle Maximus?"

"You know he will not believe that whatever he is told," Kelda said. "Stop being faint-hearted, Yvette. If you are to escape from this dreadful situation, we have to keep our wits about us every minute of the day."

"Oh, Kelda! Kelda. What would I ever do without you?" Yvette cried. "Thank God you are with me."

Kelda, as she put her arms around Yvette, also thought that it was a good thing that they were together.

She did not underestimate the task she had set herself in saving Yvette and she thought this morning when they were out driving that Lord Orsett was even more formidable than he had seemed when they had first met.

There was something about him that made her feel that he was a conqueror, a man who would always get his own way and a man who would fight to the death rather than surrender.

But it was something that she had no intention of saying to Yvette.

Before going down the stairs they both changed into elegant gowns that could only have come from Paris.

Yvette's was pale oyster-coloured lace over chiffon with a coral sash around her tiny waist and a coral ribbon around her throat. A very attractive locket set with diamonds that had belonged to her mother hung from a chain around her neck.

She looked very smart and very lovely and only because she had insisted on it Kelda was wearing an equally elegant gown of fine silk trimmed with lace that accentuated the blue of her eyes and made her skin seem almost dazzlingly white.

"I would rather be inconspicuous and remain in the background," Kelda had protested when Yvette took it out of her wardrobe.

"You know you cannot do that and have Uncle Maximus concentrating on me with eyes like a hawk. You have to distract him and keep him interested so that I can think about Rémy and watch out for him."

"You must not do it too obviously," Kelda advised her.

"How can I help it?" Yvette asked with a little sob. "It just feels as if five centuries have passed since I last saw him."

A servant led them into an even more magnificent Reception room than the one they had used previously. It was, Kelda felt very sure, kept for the most formal occasions and special guests.

It was not only the décor of the room that she admired but the beautiful arrangements of flowers everywhere that scented the air with their fragrance.

They had no sooner joined Lord Orsett than a servant opened the door and his Lordship then hurriedly went from the room.

"Where has he gone?" Yvette asked in surprise.

"I think," Kelda replied, "that it is correct for him to meet the Governor-General at the front door."

Yvette came a little nearer to her.

"I am trembling, Kelda. I know it is stupid of me but I am so frightened – frightened that you will not be able to save me and in the end I shall have to do what Uncle Maximus wants and marry this terrible old man."

"You are not to think like that," Kelda corrected her. "You have to believe that you will win. Trust in your faith and love. Say a little prayer in your heart and you will feel better and more confident."

"I *am* praying – I am praying all the time to St. Jude, the Patron Saint of lost causes."

"This one is not lost," Kelda said almost savagely. "But go on praying, Yvette. We need all the Saints on our side."

There was the sound of voices outside the door and a moment later Lord Orsett came in accompanied by the Governor-General.

He was, Kelda thought, exactly how she had pictured him, short, thin and wiry with an intelligent face deeply lined with age from spending long years in the tropics. His thinning hair was already turning from grey to white.

After they were introduced to him and they had talked, she realised that he had a certain charm as well as excellent good manners.

But he was old, there was no doubt of that. Old and to Yvette, terrifying.

She, however, behaved in an exemplary manner so that no one, not even Lord Orsett, could have found fault. Although she did not say very much, she listened wide-eyed to what was said to her.

She accepted the compliments paid her by the Governor-General with a shy modesty that made him think she had never received any compliments before and said charming things about Dakar that undoubtedly pleased both him and Lord Orsett.

Again it was a performance which made Kelda think might have graced the *Comédie Française*.

Only she was aware that Yvette was trembling as she linked her fingers together in her lap so tightly that the knuckles showed white and every now and then there was a little throb in her voice as if her real feelings might overcome her.

The Governor-General did not stay for very long fortunately.

Only when he rose to go did he hold Yvette's hand longer than was necessary and said,

"It has been a great pleasure to meet you, Mademoiselle de Villon, and, as I wish you to see The Palace, your uncle has promised to bring you and your friend to dinner tonight. It is an occasion that I shall be looking forward with more pleasure than it is possible to express in mere words."

"I shall look forward to it too," Yvette replied.

There was a sudden light in her eyes that the Governor-General could have been excused for thinking was due to what he had just said, but actually Kelda was aware that at The Palace there might be a chance of seeing Rémy.

Lord Orsett escorted His Excellency out to his carriage and, when he came back into the room, he stood for a moment looking at Yvette and Kelda standing at the other end of it.

There was something searching in his expression and, Kelda noted perceptively, his eyes were a little cynical, as if he questioned to himself whether it was possible that things could be going as smoothly as they appeared to be.

"Am I to understand that you are looking forward to dining at The Palace this evening?" he enquired.

"Of course," Yvette replied, "I have heard it is very impressive."

"Who told you that?"

The question was sharp and Yvette was quick enough to realise what answer her uncle expected her to give.

She looked at Kelda with a puzzled expression.

"Who was it who told us about The Palace, Kelda?" she asked. "Was it the Captain or those kind people who chaperoned us?"

Kelda was as quick as she was,

"It was the Captain," she said. "His Excellency received him after one of his voyages and it was a gesture he much appreciated."

The suspicion died out of Lord Orsett's eyes.

"I expect after luncheon that you would both like to rest so as to look your best for the festivities this evening," he said. "But in case, Yvette, you may be thinking of renewing your acquaintanceship with the gentleman you met during your voyage here, let me tell you that I have had his name deleted from the list of those who will be presented to you."

For a moment there was an ominous silence and, because she was desperately afraid of what Yvette might say, Kelda stepped sideways and as she did so knocked over a small table that stood beside one of the chairs.

It fell to the ground with a crash spilling over an ashtray and some small ornaments that had been placed on it.

"Oh dear, how clumsy of me!" she exclaimed. "I had not realised that it was there. I do hope that nothing is broken."

"No, everything is intact," Yvette said, picking up the things from the floor and putting them back on the table.

The moment of danger was passed and Kelda drew a sigh of relief.

Only when after luncheon they went to their rooms, did Yvette burst out into a tirade of fury against her uncle,

"How dare he prevent Rémy from coming to the dinner party! What do you think he said to the Governor-General? What explanation would he give? Perhaps he has ruined Rémy's career."

"It is much better he should not be there," Kelda said quietly.

"What do you mean by that?" Yvette asked almost fiercely.

"If he was, you would have eyes only for him and all our pretence and your play-acting would be swept away from the first moment your uncle saw you together. He would not then believe for one moment that you will agree to marry His Excellency."

Yvette was still for a moment before she admitted,

"I see what you – mean."

"But you will be under the same roof as Rémy and I cannot believe that this will not be his opportunity to communicate with us in some way. Be prepared for anything, a whispered word or something thrust into your hand. I don't know what it could be, but I am sure that Rémy will take advantage of the fact that you will be there in The Palace."

"I hope so – I do hope so," Yvette murmured.

The pain in her eyes made Kelda wish that she could hurt Lord Orsett in just the same manner and he could suffer as he was making his niece suffer now.

The gowns she and Yvette wore that evening made Kelda think that they were far more suitable for a London ball than what Yvette called 'darkest Africa'.

Lord Orsett, now looking most elegant in his evening clothes, drove with Yvette and Kelda in a closed carriage to The Palace, which was indeed as impressive as Rémy had told them it was.

A huge building, much more African in its design than Lord Orsett's mansion, it had a dignity which was enhanced by the soldiers in their short-sleeved red tunics and pointed red hats.

There were only six other guests besides themselves, all of them men, and each the Head of some distinguished Office of State.

It was therefore a party of ten that sat down in the large and imposing dining room and were served with superlative French *cuisine* under the direction, Kelda learned, of a chef who had come from France and was now training native chefs to carry on when he returned to Paris.

Because they were the guests of honour Yvette sat on the Governor-General's right and Kelda on his left, while Lord Orsett was entertained by the Minister of Justice at the other end of the table.

Kelda was aware that nothing Yvette did escaped his attention.

She sent her several warning glances during the dinner when she appeared to be looking around as if Rémy might well be concealed in some corner of the room or she might see him through one of the windows.

As Kelda felt it was important to keep the Governor-General interested and unaware of the tension that Yvette was suffering from, she made every effort to draw him out on Senegal and found it was not a difficult thing to do.

He was a man who obviously had a real desire to do his best for the country and for the French Administration of it.

He told Kelda a great many things she wished to hear and she felt at the end of the dinner that he had been unaware that Yvette had answered him in little more than monosyllables.

In the French manner there was no question of the ladies leaving the room first and they all moved together back to the large salon where they had been received on arrival.

Kelda had forgotten that this was the French custom, although she now remembered her mother mentioning it once many years ago.

It was disappointing because she had half-hoped that when she and Yvette were alone might be Rémy's opportunity of joining them. But now there was no chance of that and it was with a feeling of relief after they had talked for a little in the salon that Lord Orsett suggested that he should take them home.

"It has been such a delightful evening," he said to the Governor-General, "and don't forget that you have promised to dine with us tomorrow night. We shall be greatly looking forward to it."

"Not as much as I am, my Lord," the Governor-General replied.

He looked at Yvette as he spoke and Kelda felt her heart give a frightened throb.

She knew without being told in words, in fact she was sure, that tomorrow the Governor-General would be given a chance of talking to Yvette alone.

They walked out into the hall and servants were waiting with the light gauze scarves with which they had covered their shoulders on the way to The Palace.

Kelda waited for the man to help her with hers, turning her back to him so that he should do so. Then, as she felt the wrap put round her, she also felt something hard and square being pressed into her hand.

Automatically she closed her fingers over it and a minute later slipped it into the little satin bag she carried which Yvette had lent her to go with the gown.

Once they had arrived back at Lord Orsett's house, Kelda waited impatiently for him to say 'goodnight'.

"The horses will be at the front door at seven o'clock tomorrow morning," he said. "It is a little later than I usually ride because I would not wish you to ride too far and be stiff, being unable to take much exercise on board ship."

The way he said it made Kelda feel that he wanted to add,

' – before tonight when your prospective husband is coming to dinner.'

But he did not say anything more and Yvette replied automatically,

"It will be pleasant to ride again and you can show us what it is like outside the town, which is very much more sophisticated than I expected."

"I am delighted it pleases you," Lord Orsett said

He said 'goodnight' in a perfunctory manner to Kelda and, as she walked up the stairs beside Yvette, she knew how depressed and disappointed the French girl was feeling.

She had hoped against hope to meet Rémy, but nothing had happened and they had come away from The Palace without seeing him or without him communicating with them as far as she was aware.

Only when they had reached their bedrooms and the maids had helped them out of their gowns and they were ready for bed, could Kelda carry the little satin bag into Yvette's room.

She was lying back against her pillows, an expression of despair on her face until Kelda said,

"Look what I have brought you!"

She held out the bag as she spoke and for a moment Yvette did not understand.

Then she gave a cry.

"You mean – ?"

"Open it and see."

"Oh, Kelda, I thought he had forgotten me!"

"See what he has to say or would you rather read it alone?"

"No, no, of course not. I have no secrets from you."

Yvette pulled open the bag with fingers which seemed almost clumsy as if they would not obey her will.

She took out a small square of folded paper which Rémy had written on in small writing.

Yvette read it through while Kelda waited.

Then she almost shouted in a voice that was very moving,

"He loves me! He loves me and nothing else matters!"

"What else does he say?" Kelda asked her.

"He says that we must run away together. He has heard, as you expected, not from the Governor-General but from his *aides-de-camp* what His Excellency and Uncle Maximus's plans are. He is horrified and says that he will save me or die in the attempt! "

Yvette gave a little sigh.

"Could any man be more wonderful?"

"What does he suggest?" Kelda enquired.

"He says he is making plans and will tell me about them perhaps tomorrow or the next day. He says someone will give me some flowers and I must handle them carefully because there will be a note hidden inside them."

"Does he say how you can get away," Kelda asked, "and where you can go?"

Yvette was reading the rest of the letter with a rapt expression on her face. And so after a moment she answered in a very low voice,

"He says he loves me! *I am his*! He will kill any man who tries to take me away from him! Oh, Kelda, he loves me as I love him and somehow my prayers will be answered and – I shall be Rémy's wife."

Yvette and Kelda talked late into the night and so when Yvette had read Rémy's letter a dozen times she passed it to Kelda, who knew from the passionate way he wrote that he was deeply disturbed by what he had learnt when he reached The Palace.

At the same time, she now thought, he was a man enough not to show his fears or his apprehension to Yvette.

In fact he tried to reassure her, to make her trust him and believe that everything would come right in the end, even though they might encounter many difficulties in the meanwhile.

"Why did I not think of taking a letter to him?" Yvette asked angrily.

"Because it would have been a very dangerous and very silly thing to do," Kelda replied. "We have no idea which of the servants we could trust in The Palace and, if you had written an indiscreet letter, it might have been handed to the Governor-General, then to your uncle, and we should certainly be watched and guarded more carefully in the future than we are at the moment."

"I suppose you are right," Yvette said in a small voice, "but supposing Rémy thinks I no longer – love him?"

"I think he trusts you as you have trusted him," Kelda answered, "and I have a feeling, and it is a very comforting one, that we can leave all the planning to Rémy. All we have to do is to carry out his instructions when we receive them."

"He is so wonderful," Yvette said again for the hundredth time.

Kelda was more relieved than she was.

It had been a terrible responsibility planning what Yvette should do and how she should behave, feeling that because she had to take the initiative, if they failed, it would be her fault.

Now she was only too thankful to rely on a man and because she both liked and admired Rémy and he was in fact much older than either of them, she was sure he would be successful in saving Yvette even though the odds were stacked against them.

It was, however, difficult to sleep and all Kelda could do was try to think of how Rémy could get Yvette away from Lord Orsett's house and how they could escape from Dakar, then from Senegal without being marched back by soldiers under the command of the Governor-General.

It was all a ghastly puzzle that there appeared to be no solution to.

Even when eventually Kelda fell asleep, she was restless and had dreams when she and Yvette were being pursued by mysterious figures wearing masks like those that hung on Lord Orsett's walls.

*

They were ready in the morning at precisely the time that Lord Orsett had said he would be waiting for them and they set off to ride beyond the grounds of the house to where there was no road and it was soft and sandy underfoot.

For the first time Kelda saw strange round thatched houses where the natives lived and the *Baobab* trees, which were leafless all the year round and had huge trunks and tortured contorted branches.

They gave Kelda the impression of being the victims of a terrible curse, frozen forever at the instant of punishment.

When there were a number of them standing together, she felt that they had a menacing air.

But there were other trees that were full of light and were very beautiful, the great silk cotton trees, palms, slender coconuts and bamboos and there were all the fruit trees she had expected to find in Senegal, oranges, lemons, papayas, avocados and guavas.

Browsing among them were small gazelles, antelopes and monkeys, which scurried away at their approach and occasionally, when they rode close to water, she could see a glimpse of some huge hippopotamuses.

She found it all fascinating and she knew as they turned for home that Lord Orsett was pleased at her enthusiasm.

"What do you think of my country?" he asked Yvette as she had not spoken.

"*Your* country?" she asked. "You are English, Uncle Maximus."

"It is my adopted land," he said, "and the more I learn about Africa the more I realise how much there is to learn and the more fascinating I find it."

"Do you intend to settle here for the rest of your life?" Yvette asked him.

"I expect so," Lord Orsett replied. "It will be a long time, at any rate, before my book is finished."

"Of course – " she began with a sideways glance.

Kelda knew from the tone of her voice that she intended to be deliberately provocative as she added,

"As you are so keen on increasing the white population, I expect that you, yourself, will be getting married."

Kelda felt herself gasp at Yvette's audacity, but she knew it was because she was feeling happy and reassured by Rémy's letter that she was no longer so frightened of her uncle as she had been ever since they arrived.

There was a long pause before Lord Orsett replied.

Then he said,

"The idea has certainly occurred to me, but then I have not been back to England for so long, it seemed somewhat impractical."

As he spoke, riding at a jog-trot with the girls on each side of him, he turned his head to look at Kelda and she met his eyes.

For a moment she ceased to breathe.

Then, as if she knew what he was thinking without words, she felt herself give a sudden gasp.

It could not be true.

He could not be thinking what she thought he was thinking, she told herself as they rode on.

And yet she knew unmistakably what had been in his mind at that particular moment.

CHAPTER FIVE

Seeing the Governor-General draw Yvette to the other side of the long Reception room in a somewhat obvious fashion, Kelda knew that this was what they had been expecting.

Lord Orsett continued to talk to her as if nothing unusual was happening and so she was aware that she must concentrate on him and answer him intelligently.

She would have been far more apprehensive had she not known that in what was a risky yet clever way Rémy had sent Yvette another note.

When the Governor-General had arrived, Lord Orsett had met him at the front door and brought him into the Reception room.

He came in carrying in his hand a really magnificent bouquet of orchids that on any other occasion would have been a gift to delight the recipient.

Kelda was well aware, however, that Yvette was nervous and apprehensive as to what the evening would produce and was longing irrepressibly for some further communication from Rémy.

As the Governor-General advanced at Lord Orsett's side, Kelda remembered that Rémy had told Yvette that somebody would give her flowers and she should handle them carefully.

She had not believed it in any way possible that he would be so daring as to hide a note in the bouquet that the Governor-General was himself presenting to the girl who he thought would be his future wife.

Then Kelda told herself that perhaps there was no other way that it was possible to carry a note secretly into Lord Orsett's household.

She wished that she could say something to Yvette and warn her to be careful.

Then, as the Governor-General greeted Yvette and presented her with the bouquet, Kelda was alert.

"I also have a present for you, Miss Lawrence," he said and handed her a small box tied with ribbon, which she was sure contained chocolates.

"How very kind of you to think of me, Your Excellency."

There was a little pause while the Governor-General looked at Yvette and automatically she said,

"The flowers are lovely. I am very grateful."

"I will put them in water," Kelda suggested. "As they are so beautiful, we must make them last as long as possible."

She took the bouquet from Yvette as she spoke.

"A servant can do that," Lord Orsett chimed in.

Kelda smiled at him.

"I confess to having forgotten my handkerchief," she said, "so I will give instructions to the maids when I go upstairs. I know Yvette will want these flowers in her bedroom."

Before Lord Orsett could protest further, she hurried from the Reception room and ran across the hall and up the stairs to her bedroom.

As soon as she had closed the door, she searched the bouquet and found that there was a very wide ribbon holding the stems of the orchids together.

It took her a few seconds to undo it and she discovered, as she had expected, that there was a piece of paper under it also wrapped around the stems.

She hastily hid it in her drawer, picked up a handkerchief and called for one of the maids who was outside to put the flowers in water.

Then she ran downstairs again knowing that anything that happened this evening was of little consequence.

All that mattered were the instructions that she was sure were written in the note that the Governor-General had unknowingly delivered.

It was even amusing that all unawares he had been the messenger of love. She longed to tell Yvette what she had discovered, but knew that it was too dangerous.

Only when they left the dining room walking ahead with the gentlemen behind them did Kelda manage to say to Yvette in a low voice,

"The flowers that His Excellency brought you are exactly what you needed!"

She saw Yvette's eyes light up as she looked at her and, as she smiled a wordless reply, Kelda saw a radiance sweep over Yvette's face almost like the sun rising over the horizon.

Kelda recognised that the knowledge of Rémy's note waiting for her up the stairs would make it easier for her to play her part when, as she suspected, the Governor-General would declare his intentions and she would have to make some sort of answer to him.

"You asked me about my carvings," Lord Orsett was saying, "and there are two in this room that I think are some of the finest examples I have found anywhere."

As he spoke, he walked across to a cabinet where the carvings were displayed and then pointed out the terracotta head of a man.

"This is thirteenth century," he said, "and comes from Nigeria."

"It is beautiful," Kelda exclaimed.

"Do you really think so? Or are you just saying it just because you think it is polite?"

"I am telling the truth," Kelda replied, "and I think the ivory carving is beautiful too."

"It is a pectoral mask," Lord Orsett explained.

Kelda looked at them both for some moments and then she said,

"I would be interested to know who they portrayed, but I suppose as they are so old that is impossible."

"I imagine it is one of their Chiefs or war leaders," Lord Orsett replied, "and like poetry, the carvings are in praise of him."

Kelda looked at him for more information and he said,

"I thought you might know that the praise name is the most widely used poetic form in Africa. It is applied not only to Gods but to men, animals and plants."

"How exciting!" Kelda exclaimed and she really meant it.

"I presume you are aware," he said, "that poetry in Africa exists almost exclusively in chanted form or as a song."

"I did not know that, but I can well understand the Africans finding it easier to express themselves to music more than in any other way."

She looked at the terracotta head again with its fine features, its thick-lipped mouth and what she felt had been intelligent eyes when the man from whom it had been modelled had been alive.

Because she was so entranced by its appearance she said almost as if she was speaking to her father,

"Recite me a poem, my Lord, and tell me the sort of praise name that would have been written about a man like this."

Even as she spoke she thought that he was rather surprised, but obligingly Lord Orsett answered,

"I have recently translated one that was written of the great Zulu Chieftain, Shaka, but I will not bore you with more than a few lines."

He paused and then recited in his deep voice,

"*He is Shaka, the unshakable,*

Thunderer – while sitting, Son of Menzi,

He is the bird that preys on other birds,

The battleaxe that excels over other battleaxes."

"This is fascinating," Kelda enthused. "But you say it is very long?"

"It goes on for quite a number of pages in my book," Lord Orsett replied with a smile. "*Ijaba*, the hunters' songs, usually take as long as the hunts themselves."

Kelda laughed and then she looked round to see that Yvette was coming towards them from the other end of the room.

She was not looking particularly agitated, but Kelda thought that the Governor-General had a smile of satisfaction on his lips.

"I think I should be leaving now," he said to Lord Orsett, "but I have plans for a large dinner party at The Palace the day after tomorrow."

"I am sure it will be delightful," Lord Orsett observed.

Kelda saw the sharp glance he gave to Yvette and she was sure that he was wondering whether the dinner party was to be the occasion at which her engagement to the Governor-General would be announced.

The Governor-General held out his hand to Yvette.

"*Au revoir*, Yvette," he said. "I shall count the hours until we meet again."

Kelda heard the emotion in his voice and was aware that he had called Yvette by her Christian name for the first time.

What was more, after looking at her for a long moment, he raised her hand to his lips.

She realised that Yvette gave a little shiver at the touch of his lips, but she thought it was almost imperceptible and hoped that Lord Orsett had not noticed.

The Governor-General then turned to her.

"*Au revoir*, Mademoiselle Lawrence."

"*Au revoir*, Your Excellency, and thank you for your present. It is very kind of you."

"It is my pleasure," the Governor-General said automatically.

He walked from the room with Lord Orsett beside him and only when they were out of hearing did Yvette ask in a whisper,

"There is a letter from Rémy?"

"Yes," Kelda replied, "it is upstairs in my bedroom."

Although she was afraid that they might be overheard, she asked,

"What did His Excellency say to you?"

"What do you expect he would say?" Yvette replied. "He paid me fulsome compliments and hoped we would be very happy together when we were married at the end of the month."

"What did you reply to him?"

"I replied that it had all been a great surprise to me and, although I was deeply honoured, I hoped that he would give me time to become accustomed to the idea of being married, especially to someone so distinguished."

Kelda gave a little laugh.

"That was clever of you."

"I tried to think that it was not me who was speaking," Yvette said, "but some woman in a play, a play that *must* end happily,"

"It will," Kelda said confidently.

It seemed a long time before they could say 'goodnight' to Lord Orsett and go upstairs, but as they did and Kelda thought it was rather tactless of him, he said to Yvette,

"I understand you have made my friend His Excellency an extremely happy man. I am delighted that you have seen sense and I must commend you on your behaviour this evening and last night when we dined at The Palace."

"I am relieved to hear that you are pleased with me, Uncle Maximus," Yvette answered demurely.

Kelda suddenly had the idea that Lord Orsett was going to refer to Rémy and say he was relieved that what he had called 'a shipboard romance' was over and finished.

Because she did not dare to trust Yvette's reactions to this, she said quickly,

"I think, my Lord, as we are both tired and somewhat stiff from riding this morning, it would be wise for us to get our beauty sleep."

"I am sure you are right, Miss Lawrence," Lord Orsett replied. "Goodnight."

"Goodnight, my Lord."

"Goodnight, Yvette," Lord Orsett said, "and I think you are growing to appreciate the attractiveness of Senegal. As it is to be your future home, there is a great deal more I want to show you. Perhaps tomorrow morning you will feel well enough to ride a little further than we did today."

"That would be delightful," Yvette answered. "Goodnight, Uncle Maximus."

She turned away with an eagerness that was irrepressible and because she was moving so fast Kelda slipped her arm through hers to force her to go more slowly.

She had a feeling that Lord Orsett might be more perceptive than they gave him credit for and he might remember and think it strange that she had taken Yvette's bouquet from the room herself rather than order a servant to do so.

"Be careful," she warned Yvette under her breath and then said aloud,

"I personally am feeling very stiff. You will have to help me up the stairs now as if I was an old woman."

"It will wear off by tomorrow morning," Yvette commented.

"I hope so," Kelda replied.

They were both aware that Lord Orsett could hear what they were saying but they did not look back and continued slowly up the stairs and along the corridor that led to their rooms.

The maids were waiting and Yvette had to be patient until finally they had withdrawn and they were alone.

Then she ran through the communicating doorway to Kelda's room to ask,

"Where is it? Show me! Quickly, quickly! I shall go mad if I have to wait one second more."

"I know what you are feeling," Kelda replied, "but, dearest, you must be so careful."

She opened her drawer and then found the letter where she had hidden it and put it into Yvette's hand.

"Oh, Rémy, Rémy, I love you!" Yvette cried and kissed the paper before she opened it.

She flung herself down on Kelda's bed and, when she had read only half of what Rémy had written, she looked up, her eyes shining like stars, to say,

"Tomorrow! We are leaving tomorrow!"

"I cannot believe it." Kelda gasped. "But how? Tell me how?"

"It is all here," Yvette said. "Let me read it to you."

She sat up holding the letter in her hand and for a moment she seemed so excited that it was impossible to translate what her eyes read into words.

Then she began,

"*I love you, my dearest heart, and I know that it is imperative that we leave immediately before things become more involved and more difficult than they are at the moment.*

I am well aware that I am taking a grave risk in sending this letter with the flowers that His Excellency will carry to you personally.

The only servant I can trust in the whole place has the task of arranging them for you and he has told me it would not be safe to try to bribe any one in his Lordship's household. There is nothing I can do therefore except pray that this will reach you.

What I have arranged, and everything depends on you, is that we shall leave Dakar early tomorrow morning in an English ship that is travelling directly from here to Cape Town.

We shall be safe once we go aboard because the French will have no jurisdiction over an English ship. We can be married at sea by the Captain and then you will be my wife. And, as it will be a long time before we find our way back to France, it will be impossible for Lord Orsett, or anyone else, to undo what has actually been done."

Yvette gave a little sigh of happiness.

"What he means is that it will be impossible for them to say that the marriage was null and void because I have not had my Guardian's permission. And by that time I might easily be having a baby!"

Kelda was surprised at the way she reasoned it out, but she waited for the next part of the letter, wondering how Rémy was going to arrange Yvette's departure from the house.

"He then writes a lot of very loving things about what he will feel once we are married, but this is the important part – "

She read on,

"As I have ascertained for, as you can imagine everything one does is known in Dakar, your uncle goes riding every morning and today you and Kelda went with him. Tomorrow he will doubtless leave at

the same time, seven o'clock, but you must be unwell and Kelda will go with him alone.

The moment that they have left and from some place of concealment I shall be watching them ride away.

I will then arrive at the house with a carriage to tell the head servant that the Governor-General has been informed that one of your relatives is dangerous ill and you have to leave immediately for France.

You must be absolutely ready and join me the moment I step into the hall. We will then rush to the quay and board the ship a few minutes before she sails at seven-thirty."

Kelda gave a little gasp and Yvette sighed,

"Can anyone be as clever as Rémy? You do see that the servants will be too bemused to do anything but what he says? And we shall be far away from Dakar before you and Uncle Maximus return from riding."

"It sounds as if it might work," Kelda reflected. "What about clothes?"

"Clothes!" Yvette exclaimed.

Then she threw up her hands saying,

"Of course! Rémy has forgotten about them! How can I go to Cape Town with nothing but what I stand up in?"

Kelda did not reply and after a moment she said,

"But nothing matters. I will go naked if it means I can marry Rémy and never see the Governor-General or Uncle Maximus again."

"Wait a minute," Kelda suggested. "I have an idea."

"What is it?"

"We can hardly ask for a trunk to be brought to our rooms. It would certainly seem very strange and your uncle might be told about it, but there is nothing to stop you being extremely unconventional and taking your clothes with you wrapped up in sheets."

Yvette stared at her for a moment in a bewildered fashion and then she gave a little cry of joy.

"Oh, Kelda! *Kelda*! You are so clever. Of course I can do that. The servants will think it odd, but it does not matter what they think. We will have everything ready here and just as Rémy is watching you ride away from the outside of the house, I will watch from the inside. Then I will make the maids carry down the bundles and we will take them with us in the carriage."

Kelda and Yvette rose to their feet and then Kelda had another idea.

"We have to convince Lord Orsett that you are not well enough to go out riding. It would therefore be wisest when the maid comes to call you that you should be in bed. So we must use my sheets and not yours."

"Do you really think if they thought I was pretending to be ill or tired, they would tell Uncle Maximus?"

"It would certainly be taking chances," Kelda said. "You have no idea whether or not he is spying on you and it would be a mistake to underestimate his intelligence."

She paused for a moment concentrating with a little frown between her eyes before she said,

"He is certainly surprised at your being so sensible and since that first night you have made no mention of Rémy even though you claimed that you were engaged to him."

"We have been banking on his not knowing much about women," Yvette remarked.

"He is still a very intelligent man," Kelda answered. "He is not as suspicious as he was, but I cannot believe that he does not think it curious that you have accepted the Governor-General's proposal without a protest and without even suggesting that the marriage should be delayed for a further month or so."

"I see what you mean," Yvette pondered. "Perhaps that was a mistake."

"Now it is immaterial one way or the other. At the same time you must not put a foot wrong. The maids will call us as they have every morning at half-past six and only I will be already up. You will take no notice when they draw back the curtains and I will go down the stairs and tell your uncle how tired you are and that you would rather spend the morning in bed."

"So we will have to make do with just your two sheets instead of four," Yvette said in a practical manner.

It took them a long time to place all Yvette's most expensive and attractive gowns in the sheets and fasten them with safety pins so that they could be carried easily to the carriage and from the carriage to the ship.

Only when there was no room for anything else, they decided that they could use also the bottom sheet on Yvette's bed.

In this they packed her hats and sunshades. A pillowcase was filled with her shoes and, when everything was complete, the huge white bundles were hidden in Kelda's wardrobe.

Yvette flung her arms around Kelda's neck to say,

"Thank you, *thank you*! Oh, dearest Kelda, if I really do get away tomorrow, I shall be eternally grateful to you for the rest of my life."

"You have to get away," Kelda said. "If this fails, I am sure you will never have another opportunity of escaping."

"I know," Yvette murmured, "and for the rest of the night I shall be praying."

She went to the window as she spoke and looked up at the stars in the sky as if she was already speaking to God and invoking His help.

"I know one thing, Kelda," she now said, "that if Rémy and I have to be married by the Captain of an English ship, we will as soon as we reach Cape Town find a Catholic Church in which we can be married according to our own religion."

"I feel sure that Rémy has thought of that already," Kelda smiled.

"He thinks of everything. Are you surprised that I am so overwhelmingly in love with him?"

"I think he is very clever and you are very clever too," Kelda replied, "and, when he is Prime Minister of France, you will obviously make him just the sort of wife a Prime Minister should have."

They both laughed a little tremulously, but their tears were very near the surface.

Then Yvette hugged Kelda again and, as they both knew that it would be wise for them to rest before the excitement of tomorrow. they went to bed.

*

It was impossible to lie still knowing that everything depended on Rémy's planning and there being no setbacks at the last moment.

She had the terrifying feeling that quite unexpectedly Lord Orsett might well decide not to ride this morning or that, as Yvette would not accompany them, they would be delayed in leaving the house and the ship would sail before Rémy and Yvette could reach the quay.

There were hundreds of things that could happen and Kelda found it impossible to lie still. So she rose and dressed herself in the attractive thin riding habit that Yvette had lent her and put her hat, whip and gloves ready on the bed.

At six o'clock she went into Yvette's room to find her, as she had expected, half-dressed.

"If I lie under the bedclothes when the maid comes in," she explained, "she will not be aware of what I am wearing."

"My maid usually knocks at my door first," Kelda said, "so I could prevent yours from pulling back the curtains and tell her that you wish to go on sleeping."

"Suppose they tell Uncle Maximus and he then decides not to go riding?"

"Yes, of course, you are right," Kelda said. "We must behave quite normally. You just feel sleepy and let her put out your things for you as usual."

As soon as she spoke, she gave a cry of horror.

"I had forgotten your wardrobe is empty! Oh, Yvette, we must think of everything. If we make a mistake now, we are lost."

"I have already thought of that," Yvette said, "and as you see my riding habit is on the chair and I have put what I shall wear in the wardrobe and locked the door to be quite certain she cannot open them."

"You are cleverer than I am," Kelda said humbly. "My only excuse is that I have not had so many clothes to worry about as you have had in the past."

"You will be glad to know that I am leaving you still more," Yvette said, "And after all you have done for me, when you join me in Paris, I will give you the most wonderful gowns any girl has ever possessed."

"When do you think you will be in Paris?" Kelda enquired and Yvette, hearing the now serious tone of her voice, said,

"I know, dearest Kelda, that you are thinking that Uncle Maximus may send you back immediately to London in disgrace. Here is all the money I brought with me, which is enough to take you to Paris."

She paused and went on,

"As Rémy suggested when you get there you must go to my aunt's house and wait for me. I shall write to her, and post the letter the moment we arrive in Cape Town, to tell her what has happened. But here in the meantime is a note which will introduce you and say how important you are to me."

"How can you think of *me* at a time like this?" Kelda asked her.

"Of course I think of you because I love you," Yvette replied. "If it had not been for you and the clever way you have made me act a part in front of Uncle Maximus, I am sure by this time I should have been incarcerated in a dungeon or locked up in an attic where Rémy could not reach me."

"I would not wish to be a – burden or a – nuisance to you," Kelda admitted.

"You will never be that," Yvette said. "Rémy and I will look after you and one thing I do promise, you will never go back to that horrible old dragon in the Seminary to be bullied as you were before we came here."

The tears ran down Kelda's cheeks as she kissed Yvette.

Then as if she realised that the only thing that mattered at the moment was for Yvette to be ready when Rémy came for her, they both took up what Kelda called their 'battle stations'.

Everything went smoothly, the maid came into the room to pull the curtains and Yvette said in a sleepy voice,

"I will not get up for the moment. I will call you when I wish to do so."

The maid left the room having put a tray containing coffee and a warm *brioche* beside the bed.

Kelda had the same and she carried her cup of coffee into Yvette's bedroom.

"You had better eat something and drink your coffee," she said, "otherwise you may feel faint."

Yvette smiled.

"Not if I know I am going to see Rémy. In fact I already feel as if I have drunk a whole bottle of champagne and am floating towards the sky."

"You may feel like that, but only when the ship has actually moved out of Port," Kelda said.

She finished dressing, kissed Yvette fondly goodbye, then at exactly ten minutes to seven she walked from her bedroom and spoke to the maids who were waiting in the corridor.

"Mademoiselle is fatigued this morning," she said, "and has decided not to go riding. But please listen for when she calls for you, she will require your assistance."

She spoke slowly so that they would understand exactly what she wanted and then went downstairs.

She and Yvette had already carried the large bundles of clothes into her room and set them ready by the door and Yvette herself was dressed in her travelling gown, waiting for the moment when Lord Orsett and Kelda rode away from the front door.

This, Kelda knew, was the crucial few minutes when she must explain to Lord Orsett that his niece would not be joining them, but she herself would like to go riding.

She knew that he, like them, had only coffee in the morning before he went riding and yesterday they had all had breakfast on the terrace when they returned.

She had no idea where he might be, but, as she reached the hall, she saw with a feeling of relief through the open door the horses coming round from the stables.

Then along the corridor that led to Lord Orsett's private room she heard footsteps and a moment later he appeared.

If she had not been so agitated and her heart had not been beating so very frantically in her breast, she would have thought, as she had yesterday, that he looked exceedingly elegant in his riding clothes.

All she could think of, however, was the part she had to play and that one slip might ruin Yvette's life.

"Good morning, Miss Lawrence," Lord Orsett began.

She thought he sounded as if he was in a good temper, perhaps because Yvette had been so charming to the

Governor-General last night and had not opposed his plans in any way.

"Good morning, my Lord," Kelda replied, "but I am sorry to tell you that Yvette hopes you will excuse her from riding this morning."

"She is not ill?"

"No, not ill but very tired and, as you had anticipated, somewhat stiff. She will join us for breakfast when we return unless, of course, you would rather I did not accompany you."

She had a feeling that just because she had suggested that he should ride alone, he would take the opposite view.

"I see no reason why you should be deprived of your exercise," Lord Orsett said almost immediately.

Kelda hoped the relief she felt did not show too obviously in her face.

"I would like to come because you promised to take us on a different ride from where we went yesterday and I hope that means I shall see some more wild animals."

"We may see some," Lord Orsett replied, "but I had intended this morning to show you both a bush village and one that I think you will find extremely interesting because it is where the natives dye the fabrics that you have already admired."

"I would love that," Kelda exclaimed. "Oh, please, let's go there."

Lord Orsett smiled and she thought that he was amused by her enthusiasm.

It was still not seven o'clock when they walked down the steps and mounted the horses waiting for them outside.

Kelda was sure that somewhere hidden amongst the massive shrubs and trees Rémy was watching them go and she wished that she could wave to him and somehow express her joy that his plan was succeeding.

Instead she merely rode off as quickly as she dared and they were soon out of sight of the house.

It was a glorious morning and the wind from the sea fanned Kelda's cheeks as they rode over the sandy soil.

She tried not to think of what was happening once they had left and forced herself when they were moving a little slower to draw out Lord Orsett on the subject in which he was most interested, which was of course, Africa and his book.

She found that this was not difficult and she started off by saying,

"I was thinking last night of the magic that everybody seems to associate with Africa. Have you found much of it in your researches, my Lord?"

"Naturally in primitive peoples superstitions and what they call 'magic' play a large part in their lives," Lord Orsett replied, "but after I had gone to bed, I remembered the incantation that I thought would interest you."

"Do recite it to me," Kelda urged him.

"An Ibo diviner, for example, invokes the truth before consulting his bones," Lord Orsett explained, "and this one I think is a particularly fine poetical effort."

He raised his chin a little as if he was looking at the unknown as he recited,

"What will it be today?
Success or failure? Death or life?
What is the evil spirit that throws his shade?

Between me and the truth?"

"I like that!" Kelda exclaimed.

She felt somehow it was particularly applicable to what was happening at this moment and wondering if in some perceptive way Lord Orsett, although he was not aware of it, had sensed that something strange was afoot.

"At the end of this incantation," he said, "there are two lines that I think are particularly inspiring,

"Here the sun rises
See the truth come riding on the rays of the sun."

"That is lovely," Kelda agreed.

There was silence for a moment.

And then she said,

"I shall look forward to reading your book, my Lord."

"The first volume is practically finished."

Kelda looked at him questioningly and there was a faint smile on his lips as he said,

"If you would not find it too difficult to read from the manuscript, then I will give it to you."

"I would love to," Kelda said sincerely.

Then she remembered that once they returned to the house there would be no question of her reading his manuscript or in fact of being there longer than it took to pack her possessions and be sent away on the first available ship.

The idea was depressing because in the short time that she had been in Dakar she had seen so little of the countryside and its people.

Thinking about how much she would miss, she rode in silence and was therefore startled when Lord Orsett asked,

"What is worrying you?"

Kelda looked at him in surprise.

"H-how do you know I am – worried?"

"I am not quite as obtuse and insensitive as you appear to think I am."

For one terrifying moment Kelda felt that he was going to say he had known all along of their plans for Yvette to escape and she was at this moment locked in her bedroom with no chance of reaching Rémy.

Instead he went on,

"I think you are an unusually sensitive person, Miss Lawrence. Sensitive people throw out an inescapable aura that can be picked up by those who are attuned to it. I know therefore that something is disturbing you."

"If it is," Kelda replied, "it is not worth thinking about in such beautiful surroundings."

She forged ahead as she spoke and exclaimed,

"Look, I am sure that there is the bush village, I can see the pointed tops of the roofs."

"You are quite right," Lord Orsett agreed. "Equally I hope that you will tell me of your trouble or worries, whatever they may be, on the way home."

Because Kelda found so many fascinating things to see in the village and, as she dreaded the revelations that were waiting for Lord Orsett when they returned, she managed to spend a long time not only inspecting the dyeing of the fabrics but also hearing some local music.

A tall, broad-shouldered young man played for her and Lord Orsett a *Cora*, the large and round calabash acting as sounding board with strings made with twisted nerve-fibres.

It made a clear rather subtle sound, which Kelda knew could make a perfect background for the chants or as part of the orchestra for dancers.

"The next thing that you and Yvette must see," Lord Orsett said as they rode back, "is the dancing. In Senegal to dance expresses every aspect of life and the dancers wear round their ankles little bells or tiny rattles made of millet seeds and wrapped in leaves."

"It all sounds fascinating."

She could not prevent her voice from sounding wistful, because she knew that she would leave Dakar without having seen the dancers and they would be only something to imagine in the future, just as in the past years she had had to imagine everything that was beautiful.

Because she thought she would be seeing it all for the last time, she looked around her as they rode home trying to miss nothing of the trees, the flowers, the fruit, the animals or the people themselves.

Plodding between the villages were the women carrying large bundles on their heads and there were men working in the fields using wooden implements that Kelda was certain went back into antiquity.

Then at last there was the sea and silhouetted against the sky the roof of Lord Orsett's house.

Now Kelda's heart began to beat agonisingly. Her lips felt very dry and it was difficult to respond to anything that Lord Orsett said to her.

Two grooms were waiting outside the front door and they went to the heads of the horses as Lord Orsett dismounted and then moved towards Kelda to help her to the ground.

She had already lifted her leg from the pommel and slipped down wishing, as she walked up the steps, that the ground would open and swallow her up.

In the hall she saw waiting beside the servants the elderly man who had met them at the ship on their arrival.

"Good morning, Bonnier," Lord Orsett said.

Kelda had the idea that there was a slight air of surprise in his voice that he was there.

"I have to inform your Lordship," Monsieur Bonnier said, "that soon after you had left a carriage arrived from The Palace with a message from His Excellency informing us that one of Mademoiselle's relatives is seriously ill in Paris and that she must leave at once on a ship that was sailing from Dakar this morning at seven-thirty."

As Monsieur Bonnier began to speak, Lord Orsett had stood listening to him and, almost as if she had been ordered to do so, Kelda listened too unable to move away.

"Mademoiselle caught the ship?" Lord Orsett asked after a pause.

"I understand so, my Lord. She had already left the house when I was informed of what had happened."

"Who came from The Palace to collect her?"

Kelda drew in her breath.

"I don't know his name, my Lord," Monsieur Bonnier replied, "but he was a young man and I think he is one of the Equerries in attendance upon His Excellency."

Lord Orsett's lips tightened and now for the first time since Monsieur Bonnier had begun to speak he looked at Kelda.

"I wish to speak to you, Miss Lawrence," he said and there was a note in his voice that made her shiver.

He walked across the hall and she meekly followed him.

He opened the door of the room that they had been shown when they first arrived.

She followed him into it, the door was closed behind her and he turned round to face her.

"You were aware that this would happen," he said sharply. "I require an explanation."

For a moment Kelda thought it would be absolutely impossible for her to speak.

Then in a low voice that she meant to be calm and unhurried but which, in fact, sounded more frightened, she replied,

"You could not be so – foolish as to believe that loving – Rémy Mendès as – Yvette does and he her that they would tamely submit to your plans for her to – m-marry someone else?"

"Who planned this – and how?" Lord Orsett demanded angrily.

"Does it matter?" Kelda asked. "They are to be married without your consent, but I don't think that there is much you can do about it, my Lord."

"I can have the ship stopped at St. Louis," Lord Orsett thundered furiously, "or at any rate, when they reach Marseilles, I will make sure that this man is arrested for abducting a minor."

He spoke so angrily that his voice seemed to echo from wall to wall.

"And how will that help Yvette, if by that time she is – having a child?" Kelda asked.

She saw by his expression that this had not occurred to Lord Orsett.

Then with a muttered exclamation, that might have been an oath, he turned around and walked away towards one of the windows.

He stood for a moment looking out to sea. Because in a way she could understand what he was feeling now that his plans had gone awry, Kelda said hesitatingly.

"I am – sorry if you are – angry, but then love – real love – cannot be suppressed or forgotten overnight – as you seem to think it can."

Lord Orsett did not move or speak and after a moment Kelda went on,

"Yvette will be happy – and because she is such a sweet and attractive person – surely you would want her happiness?"

Still there was no response from Lord Orsett until in a voice that was harsh with anger he thundered,

"Go upstairs now and change! I shall expect you to be ready to accompany me in twenty minutes!"

Kelda wanted to ask him why and where they were going, but she was too frightened.

Instead she opened the door, hurried into the hall and up the stairs.

Only as she reached the top step did she hear Lord Orsett calling for Monsieur Bonnier.

'Perhaps he is making arrangements to send me home,' she thought and felt her spirits sinking into a depression that was almost like falling into a deep dark hole.

'If I have to go, I shall be all alone again.' she thought, 'and, although Rémy and Yvette have been so kind, there is nowhere I belong – nowhere where I would feel as I have felt here – happy.'

She reached the top of the staircase and looked back to see Monsieur Bonnier hurrying in answer to Lord Orsett's call.

'What is to happen to me?' Kelda asked forlornly.

She knew despairingly that once again, as when her father and mother had both died, her world had come to an end and there was nothing left but insecurity, misery and fear.

CHAPTER SIX

Kelda went slowly down the stairs feeling as if every footstep was a tremendous effort.

The maid had had her bath ready, which she always had after riding and, as she lay in its hot scented water, she recalled how difficult it had been to wash adequately at the Seminary.

There were decent baths for the pupils but, when she wanted one, she was forced to use an ancient bathroom that had not been painted for years and which led off the kitchen.

All the water had to be heated on the stove and carried up in cans that were almost too heavy for her to lift.

The only alternative was to wash in cold water and to dry herself on small inadequate and often ragged towels that Mrs. Gladwin thought were good enough for her.

To be able to wash in comfort, to be waited on, to have her gowns pressed every time she wore them, was a joy that she appreciated more and more every day that she stayed in Lord Orsett's house.

Now, she told herself this would come to an end, together with all the other pleasures she had enjoyed and she would leave Senegal with only the memory of its beauty to cherish for the rest of her life.

Through the front door she could see the flaming red of a hibiscus blossom and beyond, clambering in exotic profusion by the gates, a riot of purple bougainvillaea.

She had felt ever since she came to Dakar that the colours of the flowers warmed her as the sun did and, when she thought of the January cold and damp in England, she shivered.

With her eyes wide and frightened she walked into the salon where she expected Lord Orsett to be waiting for her.

He was standing at the far end of the room and she felt as she walked towards him that she might be covering miles instead of just a few feet to reach him.

She could hardly bear to look at him, knowing that there would be a scowl between his eyes and he would still be as angry as he had been when she had left him.

She drew nearer and still nearer, until when she stood still he said in a harsh voice, which did not surprise her,

"I have decided to offer you a choice."

At his words Kelda glanced at him quickly and saw, as she had expected, the grimness of his face and looked away again.

"Cho – ice?" she questioned, finding it difficult to speak.

"You have connived with my niece to circumvent the plans that I had made with a great deal of forethought," he said, "and I can now take you either to The Palace or to the *Palais de Justice.*"

Kelda started and there was silence before she asked in a voice that trembled,

"You – would have me – put in p-prison?"

"You might consider it that," Lord Orsett replied, "but, as it happens, I am suggesting that you will either take my niece's place and marry the Governor-General or marry *me*!"

Kelda gave a frightened gasp, then without thinking what she was saying, she exclaimed,

"You must be mad!"

"Merely practical," Lord Orsett replied. "I brought Yvette out here for a special purpose and, since you have both seen fit to flout my authority and take matters into your own hands, you are left to make reparation for her appalling behaviour."

"It is – just impossible that you can – really mean that I should – marry the Governor-General – or you."

"That is exactly what I do mean," Lord Orsett said. "As I have already explained, it is very important for the future of Dakar that there should be more European women here in a predominantly male society and, as you qualify for the position, the choice is yours!"

"Do you really – think I would – accept such a – suggestion or agree to marry in such – circumstances?"

"I am afraid that you have no alternative. But, if you need any encouragement to do what I wish, then you might feel more inclined to acquiesce without unnecessary fuss if I concede on your agreeing not to prosecute this young man whom you have decided is an eminently suitable husband for my niece."

Kelda drew in her breath.

She realised with that he was making it quite impossible for her to refuse his suggestion of marriage.

At the same time every nerve in her body and every instinct within her told her that this was as outrageous and diabolical for her as it had been for Yvette.

How could she contemplate being married to a man like the Governor-General who was not only old but, until now, had thought of her only as the companion to the woman he really wished to take as his wife?

As for Lord Orsett –

Her thoughts stopped suddenly.

It occurred to her almost insidiously, as if someone was now speaking in her ear, that here was her opportunity to remain in Dakar, to stay with the sunshine and the flowers and to be no longer afraid of an unknown future either in France or in England.

She would be safe, at least safe from the stigma of being a 'charity child', which she had carried for so long that she felt it was branded upon her brow.

The picture of being secure seemed to flash before her eyes.

She felt as if instinctively she held out her arms to it, but she knew that such security involved accepting Lord Orsett himself, so angry with her because she had helped Yvette to escape and more frightening and overwhelming than she had imagined any man could ever be.

His voice broke in on her thoughts.

"Well? Have you made up your mind?" he asked. "I imagine that you would find your position as wife of the Governor-General influential and important enough to compensate for any other shortcomings he may have."

She knew that Lord Orsett was sneering at her with that cynical note in his voice that she found more frightening than when he raged in anger.

She clasped her hands together and found that they were both cold and trembling.

"Do I – really have to – make a – choice?" she asked in a voice hardly above a whisper.

"Alternatively you can leave and return to England and then I will deal in a way he richly deserves with young Mendès!"

From the way he spoke, Kelda knew that it was just no use appealing to Lord Orsett for mercy or understanding.

She had thought when she first saw him that he was a conqueror, a man who always got his own way and a man who would win over any opposition by sheer force of character.

If he said that he would punish Rémy, he would certainly do so and she knew it would be unthinkable for her to destroy both his and Yvette's happiness.

Moreover, although perhaps it was a selfish idea, she knew that if they were parted and if Lord Orsett should be instrumental in sending Rémy to prison, then there would be no place for her in Paris.

In which case, she must go back to the Seminary and endure the life of servitude she had lived before she came to Senegal.

As if he was impatient for a decision, Lord Orsett then drew a watch from his waistcoat pocket and looked at it. Then, as he replaced it, Kelda said in a voice that was hardly audible,

"I-I will – m-marry you."

"You are sure that is what you want?" Lord Orsett enquired.

Kelda drew in her breath.

"There is – first something I must tell you – then I think you will no – longer wish to m-marry me – and the Governor-General would certainly not accept me as his w-wife."

She thought that Lord Orsett looked puzzled.

She walked away from where she had been standing facing him to one of the windows to stare out with unseeing eyes on the glittering beauty of the sea and the vivid colours of the flowers below the terrace.

Because she felt it was almost unbearably humiliating to tell Lord Orsett what she knew he must hear, she held on to the windowsill, pressing her fingers against the wood.

She stood there for what seemed a long time before Lord Orsett's voice behind her came,

"I am waiting."

"I am not – what I – appear to be," Kelda began, forcing her voice from her lips with an effort. "I – came here ostensibly as Yvette's f-friend and companion, but I was – really sent in a very – different capacity."

She felt, although he did not say anything, that Lord Orsett was surprised at what she had said and she thought, although she was not certain, that he came a little nearer to her.

"When – my father and mother were – killed in an earthquake in Turkey," Kelda went on,"1 was sent first to an – orphanage. I was a – 'charity child'."

She could not help a little sob escaping from her lips as she said the words that had been flung at her derisively for so long and which still hurt when she had to say them herself.

"I was there for three years," she continued. "Then at fifteen I was sent as a – servant to Mrs. Gladwin's Seminary for Young Ladies."

"A servant?" Lord Orsett questioned as if he thought that he could not have heard the word correctly.

"A maid of all work, a maid who did everything nobody else was willing to do," Kelda answered. "I scrubbed the floors – I washed the dishes – and I was at the beck and call of the other servants."

She thought that Lord Orsett was too astonished to speak and because she knew that she had to finish the story, she continued swiftly,

"Two years ago I was promoted to waiting on the Mistresses – and to helping the pupils in the school with their clothes and their mending."

Because for some reason that she could not explain, she wanted to be completely honest, she added,

"I deliberately sought to ingratiate myself with Yvette de Villon as I wished to – improve my French. She became fond of me – and offered me her friendship."

She turned to face Lord Orsett and stood silhouetted in the sunshine coming through the window.

"When you – sent for Yvette to come here, nobody else would come out to Africa with her. The Mistresses refused, so I was told to accompany her, as her lady's maid on the voyage – and to return if possible – by the next ship."

Although she had turned round, she hardly dared to look at Lord Orsett's face.

She stole a quick glance at him and thought that he was not scowling as deeply as he had before.

"Whose idea was it," he asked, "that you should pose as Yvette's friend and wear her clothes?"

"I was dressed in the – drab grey garments that were identical with what I had – worn in the orphanage," Kelda explained, "and it was Rémy Mendès who thought I could

– help them to convince you that he and Yvette should be married – if I was properly dressed."

"So you expected heavy opposition from me and intended to deceive me even before you reached Africa?"

"Yvette thought you would not – agree to her marriage because she was – so young. She never dreamt in her wildest imaginings that you had planned to marry her off to an – old man whom she had never even – seen."

"Most women would consider it an advantageous marriage from a social point of view," Lord Orsett commented dryly.

"B-but Yvette was – in love."

"While for you that question does not arise."

"Do you really think any Frenchman," Kelda asked, "and they are all, I would believe, exceedingly snobbish from the highest to the lowest, would wish to take a – 'charity child' as his wife?"

"We are not, as it happens, discussing how the French feel," Lord Orsett said. "You have already said that you would prefer to marry me."

"How can you – of all people – marry a – woman who has – spent the last eight years of her life in circumstances which must make anyone in the Social world spurn her as if she was a leper?" Kelda asked with an angry note in her voice.

She felt that Lord Orsett was deliberately torturing her. She had told him the truth and now he was dangling in front of her eyes the position that she might have occupied if she had continued to deceive him and had not been so honest.

As if he guessed what her thoughts were, he said,

"You need not have told me this."

"But supposing you had – found it out afterwards? Supposing the newspapers discovered and revealed the life your wife had lived before she became – a lady?"

Kelda sighed.

"I have told you the truth – and now I suppose you will make arrangements for me to – leave as soon as there is a – ship sailing to Europe."

"So you wish to go back to England?"

Kelda almost cried out that it was the last thing she wanted to do now or ever.

Again because she thought it was right that she should be honest, she said,

"Yvette and Rémy said they would – find me a position in Paris if I would – join them there."

"Doing what?"

The question was sharp.

"Rémy Mendès has three sisters. He was sure that one of them would want me to teach her children English."

"So you would prefer to be a Governess who has to accept the crumbs from a rich man's table rather than stay here and marry me!"

There was silence as Kelda stared at him.

"Are you saying," she asked after a moment, "that – after what I have told you – after you know the truth about me – you would still – marry me?"

"I dislike my plans being upset," Lord Orsett said as if in explanation. "If you are ready, we will drive to the *Palais de Justice* where, as *La Mairie* is not yet completed, Weddings take place before the Mayor, as is compulsory under the Law in France."

Kelda stared at him incredulously.

"You are – sure that what you are – doing – is right?"

"It is what I wish to do," Lord Orsett replied loftily.

She was astonished into silence. There was nothing she could say and nothing, she felt, she could do.

She thought it could not be true and she must be dreaming that she was to be married to a man who she felt regarded her not only in anger but with distaste.

But what could she do about it?

She could not possibly allow him to prosecute Rémy and, even if there was a chance of her running away, where could she go?

He walked over the room and, as he opened the door, she passed him with her head down and too afraid to look at the expression she would see on his face.

An open carriage with a white awning was waiting outside the front door.

Kelda then stepped into it and only as they drove away from the house did she think that never in her wildest dreams had she thought that she would marry in Dakar or in such weird circumstances.

When she had seen Yvette and Rémy together, so much in love and utterly content with each other, she had involuntarily said a little prayer in her heart that one day she might find love as well.

She knew that it was something she craved because since her father and mother had died nobody had loved her and nobody except Yvette had even had the slightest affection for her.

She knew instinctively that there was something within herself that could be expressed in no other way but love.

She knew that the beauty she found in music, in the books she read and the flowers that were so abundant in Senegal were all part of an emotion that reached out from her waiting to give love and to receive it.

Now without love she was to be married and she felt as if an icy hand took her heart and squeezed it so that it was hard to breathe.

'I am to be married!' her mind told her.

Yet it was impossible to realise that it was actually happening and was not something she imagined. Womanlike she glanced down to see if what she was wearing was appropriate for the occasion.

When she was changing she had been so frightened by Lord Orsett's anger that she could think of nothing but what he might do to punish her. So she had not chosen what gown she would wear, but had left it to her maid.

Now she saw that it was one of Yvette's favourites, a pretty pink with a sash in a deeper hue that was echoed by the roses that trimmed her small straw hat.

It was in fact, if she could not wear white, the perfect choice for a bride on what should be the most perfect day of her life.

But to Kelda pink was the colour of love and for her on this her Wedding Day there was no love, only fear and apprehension.

They reached the *Palais de Justice* and Kelda saw Monsieur Bonnier waiting for them outside the impressive front door.

It struck her that Lord Orsett must have sent him on ahead to make arrangements and she was surprised that he had been so sure that her choice of husband, even before

~151~

he knew the shadow over her background, would be himself.

He had spoken as if he was quite certain that she would choose the position of wife to the Governor-General. Yet there was Monsieur Bonnier waiting and, as they stepped out of the carriage, she heard him say to Lord Orsett,

"Everything is arranged, my Lord. The Mayor is waiting to receive you."

They were escorted by an Official, who bowed very low to Lord Orsett, along a number of corridors to a part of the *Palais de Justice* that was not concerned with the Law Courts.

The Official opened the door and announced,

"Lord Orsett, Monsieur le Maire."

An elderly Frenchman, wearing the elaborate and picturesque uniform of his position, rose from behind a large desk with a genial smile on his face.

*

Driving back to the house, Kelda was acutely conscious that Lord Orsett had, since they had made their responses to the Mayor and been united as man and wife, not addressed one single word to her any more than he had spoken on their drive into the town.

She reckoned that she should say something, but felt tongue-tied because she was shy.

She was married! She was Lord Orsett's wife! It was too incredible to contemplate let alone talk about.

It could not be true that after eight very long years of misery and humiliation after being derided continuously and found fault with by Mrs. Gladwin, she was now in a position which would be envied by any of the girls in the school.

In fact they would, Kelda thought, be only too willing to change places with her.

She had heard them often talk of their own futures and always they had been concerned with marrying a man who was both aristocratic and rich.

It had never seemed that love had entered into their calculations, although they simpered and giggled at the compliments they had been paid in the holidays from the young men who tried to steal a kiss.

But where husbands were concerned it was a very different matter and they all appeared to have a very clear idea of what social position they wanted to occupy in the future.

In many cases they accepted with surprising complacency the idea that their marriage would be arranged entirely between their parents and the parents of the intended bridegroom.

Kelda had only listened with half an ear to what they were saying as her mind was very usually pre-occupied with what she was learning from the books she had borrowed.

Now the memory of things that had been said came back to her and she was sure that she had made a marriage of which any mother of a pupil in the Seminary would have approved.

'But I want – love,' she told herself and then thought that she was being too demanding.

She should be grateful, deeply grateful, that there was now no question of her having to return to London and

Mrs. Gladwin or to Paris to accept what Lord Orsett had described as 'the crumbs from a rich man's table'.

At the same time because the silent man sitting beside her was now her husband, she felt her heart pounding in her breast and her lips felt dry to the point where it was impossible to speak.

As the carriage reached the iron gates and passed through them, Kelda thought that the flowers of the crimson hibiscus were even more vivid against the white of the building than they had been when she had left.

'This is my home,' she reflected, 'something I have not had since I was a child.'

"We will have luncheon immediately," Lord Orsett said as the carriage drew to a stop by the front door. "I imagine, as you had no breakfast this morning, that you must be feeling quite hungry."

He spoke in such an ordinary conversational voice that it was easy for Kelda to reply,

"Yes, I am – now I think about it – very hungry, my Lord."

As she spoke, she wondered if, now that they were married, she should still address him as 'my Lord' and knew that she would be far too shy and embarrassed to speak to him in any other way.

Because she had no wish to keep him waiting, she took off her hat in the hall and gave it to one of the servants and, without bothering further about her appearance, she just patted her hair into place and stood waiting to see where Lord Orsett would wish to go.

"A bottle of champagne," she heard him say to the head servant, "and inform the chef we require luncheon at once."

He then walked towards the terrace and Kelda followed him.

The sun was now shining so brilliantly on the dancing waves that it was almost blinding. There was the pervasive fragrance of the many flowers and the soft trade wind blew away the oppressive heat.

She felt a sudden excitement seeping all over her, almost as if she had already drunk the champagne.

She did not have to leave!

She could stay here, she could go on gazing at the beauty all around her and so need no longer feel afraid of everything she said, because there was no more reason for secrecy and no more need to be careful.

She stood looking at the scene as if she was seeing it all for the first time and then was aware that Lord Orsett had seated himself at a table under an awning and was watching her.

She turned towards him impulsively.

"It is so lovely."

She knew that it was something she had said a dozen times to him before when they had been riding and when they had looked at his native carvings, in fact, whenever they spoke of anything to do with Senegal.

Now it was more poignant and the exclamation came from her very soul as the loveliness had become a part of her and she belonged to it.

He did not reply as the servants had appeared with the champagne. They poured out two glasses of the golden wine and then Lord Orsett lifted his as if in a toast to Kelda.

"To our future," he said and his words surprised her.

"I-I hope I may – make you h-happy," she said hesitatingly after pausing to think what she should say.

Even as she spoke, she thought that it was very unlikely.

She had a feeling that he would never be happy. His cynicism and perhaps his hate were too deeply ingrained in him.

Then she told herself that she would have to try.

It was what her mother would expect her to do, and yet she felt helplessly inadequate for the task.

What did she know about men? Certainly nothing about a man as self-sufficient as Lord Orsett. What preparation had she for the life that she was to lead now?

Humbly she told herself that she was totally the wrong person for him to have married and she was convinced that the only reason he had done so was because he could not bear to be proved wrong.

He could not allow his cherished plan to fall to bits completely and have to start all over again to find a woman who would come out to live in Dakar with him.

She thought he would also feel humiliated in having to explain to the Governor-General that Yvette had not only run away rather than be married to him but that one of his own staff had actually connived in the operation.

The situation was extremely uncomfortable for Lord Orsett and Kelda now found herself feeling quite sorry for him.

"Luncheon is served," one of the servants announced and she thought that Lord Orsett was about to say something, but instead he set down his glass and rose to his feet.

They walked down the corridor towards the dining room together.

Kelda remembered that her mother had always thought that it extremely bad manners for people to sit during their meals saying nothing and so she forced herself, because there were servants in the room, to speak of ordinary things.

"You will not forget," she began, "that you promised I might see the manuscript of your book?"

They were talking in English and those waiting on them would not understand what was said. Equally they would know that they were conversing amicably.

"I have not forgotten," Lord Orsett replied.

"How did you start your momentous task of writing a history?"

"I started by reading about Africa," he answered. "I read how the Phoenicians came here, then the Greeks, followed by the Romans, the Vandals, the Byzantines and only then the first Muslims."

"It sounds fascinating, but very hard work for you, my Lord."

"It is."

"I have always heard that the Muslim religion has a very mystic side to it."

"I can see you know more than I had expected," Lord Orsett said, "and you will therefore appreciate what I have written."

"It will be very fascinating for – me."

They went on talking about the different peoples who inhabited different parts of Africa.

She thought as they talked that he appeared to have forgotten his anger and, because she was really interested in what he was saying, she plied him with questions and then forgot for a moment that there was a strange relationship between them.

She talked to him as if to a man who could tell her so much of what she wanted to know, which indeed he could.

After coffee had been served to them and Lord Orsett had accepted a glass of brandy, the servants withdrew.

For the first time since they had sat down at the table Kelda began to feel constrained and shy.

It struck her that there were so many questions she wanted to ask about their future life together and yet she had no idea how to start.

She had the feeling that he too was considering his words and perhaps something else and she could not guess what it might be.

She only felt apprehensively that he was thinking of her and she longed to know in what way.

Then suddenly the door opened and a woman came into the room.

For a moment, because she was wearing native dress, Kelda thought that she must be a servant and barely glanced at her.

Then, as she realised that Lord Orsett had stiffened, she looked at her again and saw that the woman was extremely attractive and she was sure that she was a *métise*.

There was no mistaking the distinct trace of European in her features. At the same time her smooth coffee-coloured skin spoke of her African ancestry.

She carried herself superbly and her hair was arranged in the hairstyle of a dozen tiny plaits curled round at the end, which was characteristic, as Kelda had already seen, of many of the native women in Dakar.

She wore a *boubous* in an exquisite shade of purple and her gold jewellery interspersed with amber was obviously very valuable.

She walked to the table with an unmistakable self-assurance, her eyes on Lord Orsett.

"What do you want, Antoinette?" he enquired of her in French.

"I have been told down in the market," she replied, speaking in the same language, "that you are married. I just cannot believe it is true or that you would not have informed me of it before the Ceremony actually took place."

"I intended doing so this afternoon."

As Antoinette opened her mouth to speak again, he rose to his feet.

"As you are here," he said, "we can talk about it now in another room."

He walked towards the door as he spoke, opened it and went out without waiting for her.

She followed him without even glancing in Kelda's direction and it was impossible not to notice that she moved with such an exquisite grace that was somehow reminiscent of the gazelles that Kelda had seen when she had been out riding.

Kelda sat at the dining table as if she had been turned to stone.

So this was the woman Yvette had heard one of her cousins speaking about and whom he had said was a *métise*.

There was no doubt that was what she was and she could understand, she thought, what Lord Orsett felt about her, because she was extremely beautiful and as vivid as the flowers.

Ten minutes went by and now the excitement that Kelda had felt before luncheon and the joy of feeling safe, secure and belonging had gone.

Instead she felt a sudden depression sweep over her almost as if the sunshine was blotted out.

In response to Lord Orsett's toast she had replied that she hoped she would make him happy, but she felt now that there was no reason for her to trouble herself on his account as he had Antoinette.

It now struck her how hollow her life would be when all he required of her was that she should be simply an instrument to persuade other women, principally the French, to come out and live in Dakar.

There was nothing personally she could do for him. She was just a symbol and doubtless he would find it more and more irksome to even pretend to enjoy her company.

All these years, she told herself, while he had gained the reputation of being a recluse, he had found contentment in writing his book and with Antoinette.

Kelda thought how inadequate her own looks must appear beside those of the *métise*.

Antoinette was tall with the superb carriage of those who for generations had walked with heavy loads on their heads. She would also, because of her mixed blood, Kelda thought, have a fascination and a *joie de vivre* that had been so much like Yvette.

She had always felt that the French had a charm that the English could never emulate and Antoinette would doubtless have her father's quick wit and her mother's calm acceptance of life so characteristic of Africa.

She had also the mystery and the magic of which she and Lord Orsett had been talking about.

Kelda wondered how many years she and Lord Orsett had been together, years in which perhaps he had loved her as she loved him.

But he could not marry her even though he might long to. Perhaps secretly Antoinette had hoped he would do so, only now to have her hopes shattered with the news that he had married someone else.

Lord Orsett now came back into the room.

He seemed unperturbed and moved in an unhurried manner back to his place at the top of the table.

Kelda watched him.

What had he and Antoinette said to each other? So what had happened when they were alone?

Lord Orsett picked up his glass of brandy.

"I must apologise for that untimely interruption," he declared in his usual cynical voice. "Antoinette wanted to make sure of her money and behaved somewhat unconventionally by coming to collect it in person."

The way he spoke and the indifference that he dismissed the whole episode with made Kelda feel suddenly very angry.

Without really meaning to she rose to her feet.

"I am very sure that is – untrue," she said. "I don't know how you can – speak in such a manner of someone who – loves you. Although you may not be – aware of it – *women have hearts!*"

Her voice broke on the last word.

Then, because she could not bear him to see how deeply he had affected her, she turned and ran from the room as swiftly as her feet could carry her along the passage and then up the stairs.

One of the maids was at the top and, when Kelda would have turned in the direction of her bedroom, she said,

"This way, *madame*."

Kelda, fighting for self-controlm, was not prepared to argue but allowed the maid to lead her into a large bedroom that she had not seen before.

There was a huge four-poster bed there draped at the top with white mosquito netting in a manner which made it appear like a galleon with its sails set.

But Kelda had no eyes for the room. She only wished to be alone.

"Madame must have a *siesta*," the maid suggested.

Because for the moment she could not trust her voice, Kelda stood still as her pink gown was unbuttoned and taken from her.

Then one of the soft lace-trimmed nightgowns that Yvette had given her was put over her head and almost before she was aware of what was happening she was in bed, the blinds were lowered and the door closed quietly behind the departing maid.

It was then that Kelda put both hands over her face and, as if the mere action of doing so released the tension within her like the collapse of a dam, she burst into tears.

She cried tempestuously in an abandoned manner as she had not cried since her father and mother had been killed.

She could not really reason to herself why she was so unhappy.

It merely seemed as if once again her world had fallen apart, her dreams were shattered into pieces and everything she wished for was smashed and broken.

*

Kelda stirred, realised that she had been asleep for quite a long time and heard someone moving carefully about the room.

She opened her eyes and knew that when she had climbed into bed the sun had been hot and golden outside.

Now it was dark.

She thought at first that it was only because the curtains were drawn and then she knew it was night and the maid was lighting the candles on her dressing table.

"What time is it?" she asked.

"Seven o'clock, *madame*, and I have prepared your bath."

"Seven o'clock?" Kelda repeated stupidly.

She knew that she had slept not only because she was so desperately tired having had no sleep the night before, but also because of the dreams she had experienced earlier in the day and because she had cried to the point of utter exhaustion.

"I suppose I should get up now," she said almost to herself as if she half-hoped that there would be no need and she could stay here alone and not have to see the man who was now her husband.

"Dinner is at eight o'clock, *madame*," the maid said, "and Monsieur does not like to be kept waiting."

The maid's words, spoken in halting French made Kelda climb wearily out of bed.

Her bath was cool and refreshing and she washed her face in cold water in the hope that it would erase any signs of her tears.

Then she told herself that he would not notice it anyway after the rude manner in which she had run away and he would have gone in search of Antoinette to console him.

Doubtless they would spend their time together in the part of the house that was private to him and he would think how beautiful she was and she would amuse him and make him laugh.

Then Kelda told herself severely that she should not be thinking of Antoinette. That was the secret side of Lord Orsett's life which even as his wife she could not encroach on.

Now she could understand why he had been content to stay for so long in Africa and not return to England.

His relatives had thought that it was just because he was a recluse, but would a man have need of any other companionship when he could have somebody as beautiful as Antoinette, as Kelda made herself face the word, his *mistress*?"

Because she had lived such a cloistered and sheltered life since her father and mother had died, she had not come into contact with men, nor had there been anybody to talk to her about their ways or what they thought and felt about women.

She knew only the snatches of conversation she overheard from the giggling schoolgirls or what she read in the books that she borrowed from the classrooms and which very seldom dealt with anything to do with love.

What she had learned in travelling with her father and mother was very little, but she was aware that the men of many African tribes had four or more wives and the Sultan of Turkey enjoyed a large harem of lovely women.

It had all seemed rather unreal and not translatable into flesh and blood.

But now she had seen Antoinette and she understood, she thought, that a man would find such a beautiful woman irresistible and that she should now try to compete with her for Lord Orsett's affections was out of the question.

When she had dried herself after her bath and put on the few underclothes that it was necessary to wear in the evenings, her maid said.

"As Madame is a bride, she must wear a white gown this evening."

"I don't think I have one," Kelda replied automatically and she thought as she spoke that she felt very unlike a bride and the dark cloud of despair still hung over her.

Her eyes too felt heavy from crying and she knew that she had no wish to go downstairs and meet Lord Orsett again, feeling that he would be condemning her for her behaviour.

'What does it matter if he does?' Kelda asked herself crossly. 'Everything I have done is wrong to him. He will never really forgive me for helping Yvette to escape and he made it quite clear that I should marry the Governor-General rather than him.'

Nevertheless, when her maid brought from the wardrobe a gown that had been Yvette's, she was mildly interested.

It was a ball gown of white satin covered in tulle and sprinkled with diamanté, which she remembered now Yvette had said was too voluminous to pack.

"There is no room for it," she said petulantly, when Kelda had pointed out that it was still hanging in the wardrobe. "Besides I have never liked myself in dead white."

It certainly did not become her as the bright colours she usually wore, Kelda thought, but when the maid fastened her into the white gown she knew she looked different from how she had ever looked before. Wearing the lovely gown and with her shoulders swathed in white tulle and the diamanté sparkled with every move she made, she looked bridal.

The bodice was somewhat tight and her waist looked tiny above the swirling skirts and the maid arranged her hair in a fashionable style on top of her head and then, looking at her reflection in the mirror, she said,

"*Attendez un moment, madame,*" and ran from the room.

Kelda wondered what she was doing and, as when she returned a few seconds later with two white camellias in her hand, she understood.

The maid arranged them on top of her head and it seemed to complete the elegance of the gown although she knew that Yvette would doubtless have worn diamonds.

"*Madame est très belle!*" the maid exclaimed several times and Kelda forced a smile in response.

Only as she went downstairs feeling rather self-conscious did she wonder if perhaps Lord Orsett would be amused at her for dressing up in such an elaborate manner. He might even think it pretentious of her when their marriage was so far from normal.

As Kelda reached the hall, she had an impulse to run upstairs again and put on one of the gowns she had worn before.

Then, as the head servant came forward, she knew that she was in fact almost late since it was only a minute or two to eight o'clock and Lord Orsett disliked being kept waiting. She therefore followed the servant who led her to a Reception room, where he was waiting.

He too looked very elegant in his evening clothes, Kelda thought, but, if he did notice anything strange about her appearance, he did not say so.

Instead, as she walked towards him, he picked up a glass of champagne from a side table and gave it into her hand.

"I hear you have been asleep."

"I am – sorry if it was – inconvenient."

"It was very sensible," he contradicted her. "I realise that you had very little sleep last night."

She thought that he must be angry because by now the servants would have told him that Yvette had taken most of her clothes with her and they had packed them up in his sheets. But he spoke almost as if he was amused and went on,

"There is nothing more fatiguing than dramatic or unexpected situations, at least that is what I have always found."

He was, Kelda thought, trying to dispel any awkwardness that might exist between them due to Antoinette's appearance and her own outburst.

Because it was impossible for her not to be responsive in the circumstances she said with a wavering little smile,

"I-I am sorry I could not come – driving as I think – we planned."

"It was better for you to sleep," Lord Orsett replied, "and you missed accompanying me to The Palace, a visit that was slightly uncomfortable."

He was speaking lightly and Kelda looked at him in surprise.

"His Excellency was extremely disappointed," he said in reply to her unspoken question, "but he congratulated me warmly and wishes to give a large dinner in our honour as soon as you feel that you can face such a gastronomic exercise."

Kelda gave a little laugh as he had obviously intended for her to do and then dinner was announced and they walked into the dining room.

As she entered the room, Kelda stood still in amazement.

The last thing she had expected was any kind of celebration of their marriage, but the room had been transformed with garlands of white flowers hanging from the walls and great banks of them arranged in the corners of the room.

The table was all white with the same camellias as she was wearing in her hair and on another table at the far end of the room was a large and elaborate Wedding cake.

It was all so unexpected and at the same time, for someone who had never been given a celebration of any sort in her life, an irrepressible excitement.

"H-how – could you – think of it? How could you do anything so – marvellous?" Kelda stammered

"I hoped you would like it," Lord Orsett said simply.

"Of course I like it," she replied. "But – the cake – how could one have been baked so quickly?"

"I have to admit that was bought and my chef has lost face in consequence," Lord Orsett smiled. "But he is completely determined to hold his own by producing a dinner that, if we eat everything he has prepared, will strain our capacity to its utmost point of endurance."

Kelda was listening and looking around with the excitement of a small child at its first pantomime.

Flowers scented the room and from the candelabra entwined with flowers the candles cast a golden light that made everything seem to have a magic she had never known before.

"Y-you did this for – me ? Really – for me?" she asked beneath her breath as if she still could not believe that it had not been meant for somebody else.

"I am trying to make up for the somewhat banal Service that took place in front of the Mayor. I believe that every woman, when she is married, wants a Cathedral, a choir and at least ten bridesmaids!"

Kelda gave a little laugh.

"I don't know one person I could ask to be my – bridesmaid."

As soon as she spoke, she thought that it was the sort of Wedding Lord Orsett must have had when he had been married to Yvette's aunt.

In thinking of Antoinette she had forgotten that he had been married before and his wife had died.

Had he loved her desperately? she wondered now. Was that perhaps why he looked so cynical and why at first he had shut himself away from the world?

Perhaps then he had sworn that he would never love again and had never found a woman who could equal in any way the Frenchwoman who had born his name.

'If I was French,' Kelda thought miserably, 'perhaps I could make him happy.'

She looked at him quickly from under her dark eyelashes and thought that no man could look more distinguished or more handsome.

His eyes met hers and there seemed to be a strange expression in them that she did not understand but told herself it was because the light from the candelabra distorted everything.

At the same time she was well aware that her heart was beating in a strange manner and, although she could not quite understand it, the cloud of depression that had hovered over her ever since luncheon was lifting.

CHAPTER SEVEN

As the long and elaborate dinner ended, the head servant, before he withdrew, spoke to Lord Orsett in a low voice, who nodded and then he turned to Kelda,

"The staff want to wish us happiness in the future, but, as they are Muslims, they cannot drink our health. I think therefore, we should divide the Wedding cake amongst them."

"I am sure they will enjoy it," Kelda agreed.

"And since to placate the chef we will have to eat the one he is baking tomorrow, we can just cut this one in traditional fashion and let it be taken outside."

Lord Orsett rose from the table as he spoke and Kelda, knowing it was expected of her, walked to join him at the side table where the large Wedding cake was arranged.

It was a typical French confection of white icing with a large silver bell on top and silver horseshoes and imitation orange blossom decorating each of the three tiers.

The head servant produced a long sharp knife and handed it to Kelda.

As she took it, looking rather helplessly at the cake and wondering whether she should start with the top tier or the bottom one, Lord Orsett suggested,

"I think, if we are to be correct, we should cut it together."

He put his hand over hers as he spoke.

At the touch of his fingers and because he was so near to her Kelda felt an odd sensation flash through her.

It was, she thought, half-pleasure and half-pain and unlike anything that she had ever felt before.

It was the first time that Lord Orsett had touched her except for the moment when he had placed the Wedding ring on her finger in front of the Mayor.

Then she had been too bemused to be conscious of anything except to believe that she must be dreaming.

Now she was acutely aware of Lord Orsett and the nearness of him.

Guided by his hand she thrust the knife into the bottom tier of the cake and, when it had cut through to the large silver tray on which it was standing, he said,

"I think we have performed our part. Now it can be taken away and given to those who I hope will enjoy every mouthful."

With an effort because she was shy at what she was feeling, Kelda enquired,

"I know it would be – impossible for me to – eat any more than I have done already."

"I feel the same," Lord Orsett agreed, "so let's go into a salon. Tonight we will sit in the one at the far end of the house."

Kelda wondered vaguely at his choice, but when she entered the room she saw that it too had been decorated with white flowers, not with the same profusion or with garlands as in the dining room, but there were huge vases on the tables and the scent of lilies filled the room.

"Thank – you," she said, feeling almost overwhelmed because he had been so thoughtful.

She walked to one of the tables on which there was a beautiful arrangement of camellias and stood looking down at them.

She was aware that Lord Orsett had walked across the room behind her and was now standing only a few feet away from her.

"Why have you been crying?" he asked.

Because he spoke so gently and in a voice that was different from any she had heard him use before, she felt the tears come into her eyes again.

'It must be because I am tired,' she thought, but she knew that was not the reason why she had cried so desperately and despairingly before she fell asleep.

When she did not reply, Lord Orsett said after a moment,

"I have a present for you for I feel that you should have one on your Wedding Day."

As he spoke, Kelda saw as if she was looking at a picture, the amber and gold necklace that Antoinette had worn around her neck and then, without considering her words, speaking impulsively, she said quickly,

"I don't – want a present. Please – don't give me – anything!"

She felt that Lord Orsett was surprised although she did not turn to look at him, knowing if she did, he would see the tears that were making it impossible for her to see the camellias.

"Why do you say that?" he asked.

Then after a moment, as if he had found the reason for himself, he said,

"I think I have a lot of explaining to do. Suppose you sit down, Kelda, and listen to me?"

He paused for a moment before he added,

"It is important for our future *together*."

There was just a pause before he spoke the last word and Kelda drew in her breath.

At least he intended that they should have a future together even though so much of his life would never be hers.

Obediently and still not looking at him, she moved towards one of the large sofas and sat down in a corner of it.

He chose a chair opposite her and she had the uncomfortable feeling that from there he could watch her face and know what she was feeling. Because she did not wish him to see too much, she looked down at her hands which she clasped in her lap.

There was silence and it flashed through Kelda's thoughts that Lord Orsett had changed his mind and would not after all explain anything to her.

Then he said very calmly in what she felt was a deliberately impersonal voice,

"You know from Yvette that I was married to her aunt, Ginette de Villon?"

It was a question, but Kelda would not trust herself to speak and so she merely nodded her head.

"I am sure that you must have wondered, and certainly Yvette did, why having married someone so attractive who loved the gaieties of Paris, I brought my wife to Dakar and made her stay here until she died."

There was something in the way Lord Orsett spoke that, even though his tone was quiet and calm, told Kelda that he was finding it hard to speak of the past and she had the feeling that he had not confided in any one in such a way before.

She thought that she might be wrong until he went on,

"Nobody except my wife was aware of my real reason for coming here and I have never until this moment revealed it to anyone."

Because she felt embarrassed for him, Kelda said quickly,

"I shall understand – if you do *not* wish to – tell me."

"It is your right to know," Lord Orsett replied, "and I am determined that there should be no secrets between us."

Kelda looked at him in some surprise for it was something that she had never expected he would say. Then as he went on she looked down once again at her hands.

"I fell in love with Ginette when I met her in London. I found her fascinating and quite unlike any of the young women I had met at balls and Receptions who were approved of by my mother as being eminently suitable to be my wife."

Lord Orsett's lips tightened for a moment before he carried on,

"It was what was called 'a whirlwind courtship' and, because I was young and idealistic and inexperienced, I did not think it strange that when I first met Ginette she appeared not to take the slightest interest in me and suddenly and overnight, changed completely and became as much the pursuer as the pursued."

Now there was definitely a bitter cynicism in Lord Orsett's voice and a note too as if he mocked at himself.

"I was too happy to be critical or inquisitive and the moment we were engaged we went to Paris where I was accepted most effusively by the de Villon family. We were married, had a short honeymoon and then returned to London."

Kelda was listening intently and she knew by the inflections in Lord Orsett's voice how difficult he was finding it to relate to her what had happened.

"It was some time before I understood my wife's partiality for London and also why our marriage had taken place in such haste."

Again he paused.

"No one actually told me the truth, it was just a look, a laugh, an innuendo and the fact that, when I came into a room, there always seemed to be a sudden silence as if the people in it had been talking about me."

Bitterly he went on,

"My 'Fool's Paradise' did not last for long. In the Marlborough House Set in which we moved, it would have been impossible for anything to remain a secret for long. There were always too many people involved and they talked and talked."

Kelda glanced up at him curiously. The lines on his face were deeply etched as if even speaking of what had happened brought back the pain and what she knew were the lines of disillusionment.

"I think I must have been married for two months," Lord Orsett said after a pause, "when I understood the reason for Ginette's eagerness to become my wife."

As she felt that she must know the answer, Kelda asked in a voice just above a whisper,

"What – was it?"

"She had met the Prince of Wales, the Heir to the Throne, in France. She had become infatuated with him or rather with his position and the glamorous aura that surrounded him. She then followed him to England, determined to have what she considered the honour of becoming his mistress."

"Oh – no!" Kelda murmured.

"The Prince, however, made it clear that he never indulged in love affairs with unmarried women. All his mistresses were married with complacent husbands. That was the part that my wife had assigned to me in this drama."

Kelda drew in her breath.

Whatever she had expected to hear, it was not this.

"When I learnt the truth, the whole truth," Lord Orsett said harshly, "I told Ginette that she had been mistaken, that I not only refused to be placed in such an invidious position but I would not allow anyone who bore my name to disgrace it."

For a moment Lord Orsett's voice seemed to ring out in the flower-scented room.

Then he continued more quietly,

"I had heard of Dakar. I was also already interested in Africa, then a little-known part of the world. I brought Ginette, despite her protests, out here and she died two years later."

His voice seemed to die away into the shadows and there was a silence until Kelda said very softly,

"I am – sorry. It must have – hurt you a great deal."

"I suppose 'hurt' is the right word," he replied, "but it was my pride that suffered most. I could not bear to be sneered at, laughed at behind my back or treated to the winks and nudges that other men in the same position endured. When Ginette died, it would have been possible for me to return home, but by then I did not want to go back."

"So you – stayed to write your – book."

"I began my research for it," Lord Orsett corrected. "I travelled all over Africa, meeting different tribes, living with them, learning a great deal about their customs that nobody had ever known before."

"It must have been very – exciting."

"I had built this house," Lord Orsett went on, "and, when it was finished, I found I liked being here and I enjoyed the isolation. I no longer missed the friends I had known in England. When I wanted companionship, there were always intelligent men like the Governor-General to talk to."

He paused.

The word, 'companionship' made Kelda think of Antoinette and, as if he knew what she was thinking, Lord Orsett said after a moment,

"You have by now realised that the French understand better than the English that a man, whatever his position, needs a woman in his life."

Kelda found it hard to breathe.

Of course Lord Orsett, being so handsome and attractive, had wanted women and they had wanted him.

She could see almost as if she stood in the room the beauty and grace of Antoinette, the strong outline of her features, the golden texture of her skin against the purple *boubous* and the jewelled necklace, which Lord Orsett must have given her.

Then, as once again she knew that feeling of despair and agony which had made her cry when she had gone up to her bedroom, she felt that she could not bear to hear him telling her how much Antoinette meant to him and how, even though they were now married, he could not give her up.

She had a feeling that he would ask her to be sympathetic, to accept the fact that their position as man and wife was not an ordinary one and accustom herself to the French way of life.

She remembered now reading about the Kings of France, who always had both a wife and a mistress and that such a situation was accepted not only by the Court but by the French nation as a whole.

She felt, however, that she might cry out that she just could not bear it and that it was something she could not endure.

To control herself she clasped her fingers together with such intensity that they hurt and she forced herself not to move as Lord Orsett went on,

"Because Dakar, like the many other French outposts, is isolated from Europe and even news of their relatives is much delayed in reaching those who live here and that is why the Government and the Companies the men work for recommend marriage to local women."

He paused.

"Those who do not marry have, of course, mistresses and the arrangement, as I told you and Yvette when you arrived, has certain business-like rules attached to it, which are strictly adhered to."

"I remember – that," Kelda murmured.

"The *métises* with their French blood make it easier for the more fastidious men to accept them because many are in fact well educated, while the majority of the natives are completely illiterate."

So Antoinette, Kelda thought, was clever as well as beautiful.

It was what she might have expected where Lord Orsett was concerned and she thought that perhaps there was nothing original in thinking that she might be of help to him with his book when Antoinette would know a great deal about the local tribes and could be of real assistance to him.

She could doubtless supply every detail he required on all the subjects that interested him and, if he travelled away from Dakar, she could go with him.

Kelda thought with dismay that her very last hope of being able to help Lord Orsett lay smashed, as were her other dreams and ideals.

Again she wanted to say that there was no point in her hearing any more.

He would make it very clear that there was no part for her in his life except as a woman who would sit at the head of his table when he entertained and accompany him on Official occasions.

Otherwise she would be alone, while Antoinette shared with him everything that really mattered.

She wanted to cry out that it was unfair and that in the circumstances he should never have married her.

The pain she felt was the same pain she had known when she had first been taken to the orphanage and realised that she no longer had any identity or personality of her own and was just one of a number of faceless forgotten children.

"What I am explaining to you," Lord Orsett was saying, "is the position that Antoinette has occupied in my life."

"I-I understand that – already," Kelda said quickly.

She felt as she spoke that she could not bear to hear more and did not want to listen to what he had to tell her of what the *métise* had meant to him and how it would be impossible for him to give her up.

Lord Orsett ignored her interruption and merely carried on,

"Antoinette had no right to come here today and I told her so. But she has enough French blood in her to be very shrewd, business-like and calculating where money is concerned."

Kelda raised her head wonderingly.

"Antoinette has been with me for three years," Lord Orsett said, "and during that time she has been assiduously accumulating every penny I have given herm, so that as soon as our liaison was over, she could marry another *métise*, who has also been saving so that they can start a shop together."

Now Kelda stared at Lord Orsett in astonishment.

"You mean – even while she was with you – she wished to – marry someone else?"

"I have just told you, these things are well arranged in Dakar and in all French Colonial communities. Antoinette was intelligent enough to know that the one thing she needed was money and the easiest way to obtain it was to become the mistress of a rich man."

"But – she must have – loved you?"

"I don't think that the word has ever occurred to her where I am concerned," Lord Orsett replied. "She found me generous, I provided her with comforts she would not otherwise have had and she was very discreet. That is, of course, understood in the arrangement between a man and his mistress the world over."

As if he thought that Kelda still did not comprehend what he was saying, he explained further,

"It is a mistress's object to get as much from her protector as she can. They both accept that when the arrangement is over there will be no hard feelings and no recriminations. The man pays for the pleasure he has had, but that is all. It finishes without dramatics."

"And – Antoinette does not mind – losing you?"

The question was hardly audible, but Lord Orsett heard it.

"I doubt if she will ever shed a single tear on my behalf," he said with a smile. "In fact I would be very surprised if she is not at this moment celebrating with her young man because the large sum of money that I gave her this afternoon will enable their marriage to take place immediately."

"I-I don't – understand," Kelda said almost to herself.

It was impossible to sit listening to Lord Orsett any longer and she rose from her seat and walked to the window pushing aside the curtains so that she could look out.

The window was not closed and, although it was much cooler than it had been during the day, the night air was warm and moist.

Outside the moonlight was silver on the sea and the sky glittered with stars.

But Kelda was looking into her heart and wondering why the things Lord Orsett had told her seemed suddenly to have melted away the heaviness that she had felt, which had grown and grown in her breast until she had been almost stifled by it.

Then, as she stood there, she felt Lord Orsett close behind her.

"I have made my explanations," he said quietly, "and now I think it is only fair that you should explain two things to me."

"What – are – they?"

"First, why you have been crying and second why you told me that women have hearts."

Again because his voice was so quiet and gentle, she found herself too moved to answer him and after a moment he said,

"That they have hearts was something that I thought only existed in romantic fiction. As I have just told you, the women I have known have used me for their own ends. That I am therefore diabolical, as you once said I am, is surely no surprise."

"I am – sorry I said that," Kelda murmured. "It is – not true."

"Women have hearts," he repeated ruminatively. "I would so like to see some sign of it. Have you a heart, Kelda?"

"I hope – so."

"I meant, of course, where I am concerned. What do you feel about me?"

His question Kelda felt was quite impossible to answer and she tried wildly to think of what she should say.

And then Lord Orsett went on,

"I expected you to say that you would marry the Governor-General. After all his position is far more important than mine. He would also be likely to die sooner and leave you a rich woman."

"Do you – imagine that I would ever – think of something like that?"

"Being you, I suppose not," Lord Orsett replied, "but I am sure it is the way that most modern women would think."

"Only the women – you have known," Kelda said. "I believe that women want to – love a man for – himself and not for what he can give them."

"And you have known many women like that?"

"Yvette would not marry for money, she would have married Rémy even if he had not a penny to his name."

"And you are like her?"

Kelda did not answer and after a moment he insisted,

"You have not answered my other question."

"I don't – know what you – asked," Kelda responded almost defiantly.

"You are not very good at lying," Lord Orsett said. "This morning when we were riding together I knew that something was worrying you and that you were tense and apprehensive. I admit I did not guess the reason, but I knew what you were feeling."

He was right but Kelda would not admit it and he continued,

"Then when we drove to our Wedding, you were frightened and I could understand that. On the way back your fear gradually faded away and over luncheon you were almost happy. I could feel it reaching out towards me as if you felt you had found something that you had been searching for and something that made you feel different from how you had ever felt before."

Kelda was so surprised by what he was saying that she turned round to look at him.

Now in the light both from the candles and the moonlight outside she saw an expression in his eyes that made her heart start beating furiously and she could not look away.

"But Antoinette came to see me," Lord Orsett said very quietly, "and when I came back into the dining room you were unhappy and, when you told me that women have hearts, your voice broke."

As he spoke, he came a step nearer to her and yet Kelda could not take her eyes from his.

"Then you cried," he went on, "tears that I think came from your heart, a heart that I am quite certain you have, although I would like to believe that it belonged to me."

Now once again his voice was gentle and so compelling that Kelda felt the tears well into her eyes and, before she could stop them, they ran down her cheeks.

She tried to turn away, but Lord Orsett's arms were round her.

"Are those tears for me, Kelda?" he asked. "If so, they are very precious."

She could not answer, she could only hide her face against his shoulder and he felt her whole body trembling.

His lips were against her hair as he demanded,

"I want your heart, Kelda. I want it more than I have ever wanted anything in my whole life, but I am so afraid, so desperately afraid, of being disillusioned as I have been before."

Because of the pain in his voice and because there was also a hint of fear that Kelda had never expected to hear from him, she was no longer afraid.

"Y-you – want me?" she asked. "You – really want me?"

"It is difficult to tell you how much."

"She is – so beautiful. I thought that I could mean – nothing – to you."

Lord Orsett smiled very tenderly.

"I have tried to make you understand why I have not loved anyone for many years and what I feel for you is different from anything I have ever felt before."

"Is – that true?"

Kelda was looking up at him.

The tears were still on her cheeks, but her eyes were shining and the question seemed to throb not only on her lips but through her whole body.

"I love you!" Lord Orsett said positively. "I have loved you from the moment I saw you, but I told myself it was just another illusion and there was no chance that you would care for me except that I am a rich man."

"How – could you – believe that it would – matter?"

He looked down at her, a faint smile on his lips.

Then he said,

"Tell me what I want to hear. Say it, my darling!"

The colour rose in her cheeks as she whispered in such a low voice that he could hardly hear her,

"I love – you! I know now that is why I – cried – because I thought I had – lost you and you would – never have any – use for me."

The last words were lost as Lord Orsett's lips came down on hers holding her captive.

Then, as he kissed her, Kelda knew that this was what she had wanted and what she had always longed for.

She felt as if the moon and the stars outside, the fragrance of the flowers around them and the beauty of the sunshine of Dakar were all in the sensation that Lord Orsett's kiss gave her.

At the same time there was only him and he filled the whole world and the sky.

He drew her closer and closer and his lips became more demanding, more passionate and yet Kelda was not afraid.

She thought for one wild moment that if only she could die now she would have known the perfection and glory of love that she thought could never ever be hers.

Then she knew that she so wanted to live. She wanted to live for the love she had found with the man who drew her poor, starved, hungry little soul from her body and made it his.

He kissed her until the rapture of it made her feel as if she could no longer think but only feel as if her whole body vibrated to an untamed music that could only come from God.

Then, as Lord Orsett raised his head, she gave a murmur of protest because she could not bear to lose the ecstasy that he had given her and she sighed incoherently,

"I – love you – how can I – tell you how – much I love you?"

"I just want you to go on saying it, my darling, until I believe you and you believe me and there is nothing else of any significance in the world."

"How – could there – be ?" Kelda asked.

Then he was kissing her again.

*

Kelda stirred and realised, with a feeling of inexpressible happiness running through her, that her head was on her husband's shoulder and the pale dawn sunshine was seeping through the curtains.

She moved a little closer to him and said, as if she could not believe it,

"You are – there."

"I am here, my darling one."

"How – could I go to – sleep and – lose you even for a moment?"

"I was holding you close," he answered, "and you know now that we can never lose each other again."

"Do you – still love – me?"

He smiled and kissed her forehead.

"Are you really asking me such a foolish question? But actually it is one I meant to ask you."

'That would be even – more foolish," Kelda replied. "I did not know it was possible that a man could be so wonderful – so strong and yet so gentle and – exciting."

"Did I excite you?"

She thought that there was a faint touch of laughter in his voice that she had not heard before.

Because she was shy, she turned her face against his shoulder once again.

"You – know you – did."

"Not half as much as I mean to do in the future. I have just so much to teach you, my precious one."

"You know now how – ignorant I am," Kelda said humbly. "I did not – do anything –wrong?"

His arms tightened.

"Everything you did was right, perfect and more wonderful than I can ever tell you."

"You will – teach me all about – love?"

"That is something I shall enjoy doing," he replied, "and, my darling, it is love that will teach us both far better than anything else that we belong to each other."

Kelda was silent for a moment.

And then she said,

"There is – something I want to – ask you."

"What is it, my dearest heart?"

"When you – loved me, it was more – wonderful than anything I can say in words – but did you feel – different from the way you have – felt with – other women?"

He smiled very tenderly and put his fingers under her chin to turn her face up to his.

"I shall always tell you the truth and this, my very beautiful precious wife, is true, I have never before known such pleasure as you gave me last night."

He spoke very solemnly, but Kelda gave a little cry of sheer happiness.

"That is all I wanted you to – say – because it means that I can give you – something that – no one else has – given you."

She paused before she went on,

"I felt yesterday when I was so unhappy that all over again I had nothing. I was just a – 'charity child'. But if I can give you what – no one else can do – then I am no longer poor and insignificant."

"You will never be that again ever," Lord Orsett vowed. "You have a place in my life that is more important and more essential than anything else I could ever possess."

"Do you – really mean – that?"

"I swear to you that I mean it and it is true. This is what I have missed. This is what I wanted when I was young and idealistic and thought that I would never find in this lifetime."

Kelda gave a sigh of sheer happiness.

Then she said,

"You do really – believe that if you were of no – importance and you had no money – no marvellous house, but was just an ordinary man, I should still love you as – I do now."

"That is what I want to believe, but I want you to work very very hard, my darling love, to convince me."

"I will – try – I will really try."

Kelda put out her arm across his chest as if she wanted to reassure herself that he was really there.

As if he understood, he said,

"We have many years to convince each other about our love and, while you have been sleeping, I have been making plans."

"What sort of – plans?"

"Plans to make you happy and what I know will be best for the wife who I worship and adore."

"What are these – plans?"

"Nothing frightening," he said reassuringly. "It is just that I have decided that, while we shall stay in Dakar in the winter, we will go to England in the summer."

"Oh – *no!*"

"I think it right that you and also I, who have sadly neglected my responsibilities in the last few years, should go back to the land of our birth. I will open my house in London, but I think you will be happiest, and I know I will, on the estate I own in Leicestershire."

He kissed her hair before he added,

"If nothing else, you will enjoy the horses that I intend to buy and we will ride together over the best hunting country in England."

Just for a moment Kelda felt frightened.

Then she told herself that she must think of Lord Orsett.

He was still a young man and it would be a mistake for him to bury himself away from his roots and the people he should associate with and also from his responsibilities in the County that he belonged to.

She felt that her mother was guiding her to say the right thin and helping her at this particular moment and knowing instinctively that it was a crossroads not only in her life but in her beloved husband's as well.

"Oh, darling," she said with a note of passion in her voice, "wherever we are, I would be happy with – you. I will do whatever you want, but you must help me not to make – mistakes and not to – shame you in any way."

She sensed Lord Orsett was moved by what she said, but before he could reply she went on,

"I have led such a very different life these last eight years since Mama and Papa died and I realise how ignorant I shall be of the Social world, the way to behave – what I should say – what I should do. But – if you are there and you will – teach me, I will not be – afraid."

"I will never let you be afraid again," he said. "So you must forgive me, my darling, for frightening you as I have in so many ways since you came here."

He gave a laugh and added,

"You accused me that very first evening of trying to behave as if I was God. Now you are asking me to go on doing so."

"This is different," Kelda said, "because then you were acting with indifference or hatred – but now you are acting with – love and that is what – God does."

"My precious, you have an answer for everything and I adore your clever little brain, but then I adore everything about you, your pretty face, your very revealing sensitive eyes, your lips and, of course, your body, which is now mine."

His hands moved softly across her skin and Kelda felt the strange fire that he had kindled in her last night re-awaken within her.

She thought vaguely far away at the back of her mind that she had read somewhere of the fire of love but, when she felt it, it was different from anything she could possibly imagine.

She knew as it burned within her, that what she felt was the ecstasy of love, it was what she had longed for and it could only be there if two people were joined divinely as one and was too perfect ever to be described in words.

"How can I tell you how happy I am?" Lord Orsett asked. "I want you to be so happy that you are never angry or bitter again."

He was kissing her eyes tenderly as she added,

"It is strange – but, when I was falling in – love with you, I kept thinking that you made me feel – safe and secure, which is something I had – longed for – and yet now I want to keep you safe and – protect you from being hurt or – unhappy."

"That is what you must do, my darling," Lord Orsett replied. "Now that I am so happy I realise how lonely and miserable I have been in the past. I told myself I was self-sufficient and that I wanted nothing. Then I found you and I was aware of how empty my life had been. Perhaps I have wasted these last years quite unnecessarily."

Because she could not bear him to regret the past, Kelda said quickly,

"I am certain that is not true. The book you have written will be of inestimable benefit to Europeans who want to understand about Africa and indeed to the Africans themselves."

"I would like to believe that."

"I am sure it will be true and one day your children will be very proud that they have such a clever father."

Kelda spoke without thinking and then, as she realised what she had said, the colour rose in her cheeks and she hid her face against him.

"My children!" Lord Orsett said quietly. "That is another thing that has been missing in my life."

Once again he turned her face up to his,

"Will you give me a son, my dearest love? I would like him to be born in England in the house where I was born. I would be proud to think that I have provided posterity not only with a book about Africa but with a child to carry on my family name."

"I shall – try very hard – not only to give you one son but – several."

"And a daughter as beautiful as you."

"If – that is what you – want," she replied. "But – please don't – love any of them more than me."

"I was going to say the same to you," he smiled "You are mine, Kelda, mine completely and absolutely. I shall be jealous even of my own children if they take all your attention."

"They will never do so," Kelda answered, "because it is so wonderful for me after having been alone – an orphan and unwanted, to know that I am secure and safe. I want to stay like this – close in your arms for ever and ever – "

"That is exactly what you will do," Lord Orsett replied. "I have found you, my darling, when I did not believe you even existed and I will never lose you again, *never*."

He looked down at her and, as he did so, she saw the fire growing in his eyes and felt the insistence of his hands against her body.

Then it seemed to her that the flames of the fire within her rose higher and still higher until they reached her lips and she wanted with a yearning that was agonising in its intensity for him to kiss her.

She lifted her lips and, as he held her captive, she felt as if the room was filled with sunshine, golden and glorious, and the angels were singing in Heaven

Then, as his heart beat on hers, she knew that they were *riding on the rays of the sun* into a Heaven that was all their own and would be for all Eternity.

OTHER BOOKS IN THIS SERIES

The Barbara Cartland Eternal Collection is the unique opportunity to collect all five hundred of the timeless beautiful romantic novels written by the world's most celebrated and enduring romantic author.

Named the Eternal Collection because Barbara's inspiring stories of pure love, just the same as love itself, the books will be published on the internet at the rate of four titles per month until all five hundred are available.

The Eternal Collection, classic pure romance available worldwide for all time.

Printed in Great Britain
by Amazon

22472751R00117